Trust the Terrier

A CORAL SHORES
VETERINARY MYSTERY

DL Mitchell

*June
Welcome to
Coral Shores?*

Black Rose Writing | Texas

ISBN: 978-1-68513-346-7
PUBLISHED BY BLACK ROSE WRITING
www.blackrosewriting.com

Printed in the United States of America
Suggested Retail Price (SRP) $19.95

Trust the Terrier is printed in Baskerville

*As a planet-friendly publisher, Black Rose Writing does its best to eliminate unnecessary waste to reduce paper usage and energy costs, while never compromising the reading experience. As a result, the final word count vs. page count may not meet common expectations.

Always, for Blair and Maddy

SPECIAL THANKS

So many people have encouraged and inspired me on this latest journey. They are the same people who supported my decision to go to vet school at the ripe old age of thirty. It would take a novella to name them all.

My husband, Blair, and daughter, Maddy, are my biggest cheerleaders. None of this would be possible without their unconditional love and belief that I could make it happen.

Wendy, my sister and friend, is an amazing Beta reader. I turn to her when struggling with the hard stuff. My brother, Jeff, is the creative one in the family and keeps us all laughing. My mom, Denise, is an inspiration—full stop.

I was fortunate to find the most supportive group of mystery writers and readers when I joined the Atlanta Chapter of Sisters in Crime. With Liz, Charlie, Lance, Darija, Sharon, Dawn and Angela at the helm, I've found friendship, fun and a creative, safe place.

George Weinstein, and the Atlanta Writers Club, introduced me to the world of publishing. By attending their conferences and lectures, I kept honing my skills. I've learned so much, but just enough to know how much more I can grow.

To all of my current and past clients—I've been honored to care for your furry family members. Some of you may relate to the cats and dogs showcased in *Trust the Terrier*. That's not a coincidence, since they are mash ups of my real-life experiences as a small animal veterinarian.

PRAISE FOR
Trust the Terrier

"In her heartwarming debut mystery, DL Mitchell proves you actually *can* go home again. And if you discover there's trouble in paradise, the good folks around you, including Elvis the terrier, will all do their part to put things right."
–Roger Johns, author of the *Wallace Hartman Mysteries*

"A captivating new entry in the field of Animal Cozy Mysteries. A veritable Best in Show!"
–Cathy Tully, Cozy Author, *USA Today* Best Selling Author & Silver Falchion Finalist for Best Cozy

"You'll fall in love with Elvis, the spunky little dog who is an excellent judge of character, and Emily, the compassionate veterinarian-sleuth who rescues him. I wanted to stroll the beach checking turtle nests and drink wine on the deck with Emily and her friends, helping them solve their next crime."
–Sharon Marchisello, Author of *Secrets of the Galapagos*

Trust
the
Terrier

CHAPTER ONE

"Meeeooooowwwwwww!"

"Sounds like Mrs. Pringle and Fluffy are early again," Anthony said, stating the obvious.

The first patient of the afternoon often arrived before their scheduled appointment, cutting into an already abbreviated lunch hour. Once again, Dr. Emily Benton, Anthony and the staff would be lucky to grab a few bites of a granola bar. It was par for the course when working in a small animal hospital.

"We don't want to keep them waiting since Fluffy gets all worked up in her carrier. The last time, it was almost impossible to examine her," Emily said.

"I've got this, Doc. Fluffy and I are friends now, and she's only scheduled for an ear cleaning today. Her follow-up exam with you isn't until next week. Don't forget, we need to squeeze in that house call this afternoon with Mrs. Klein and Elvis."

"Okay, Anthony. Thanks. I have a few calls to return, and then we can leave. I'll let Mrs. Klein know we should be there on schedule. You know her views on punctuality."

Today was one of those days that made Emily wonder what she was thinking when she became the sole owner of the Coral Shores Veterinary Hospital. Without a doubt it was her dream come true, but maybe it had come too soon in her career since she'd only graduated from vet school two years earlier. Too late to turn back now.

It wasn't long before Anthony was standing in the doorway of Emily's office, demonstrating he still had all ten fingers intact. "Everything is good with Fluffy. I think her ear infection has finally resolved, which could explain why she's in a better mood. I've got the mobile vet kit packed up in your car. Ready when you are."

"Good timing. I just finished my last call. Let's go."

• • •

It was a short drive from the hospital over to Gulf Beach Road, where Mrs. Klein lived. Coral Shores was a sleepy oceanfront hamlet on the Gulf of Mexico. White, powdery, sand beaches and the uniquely shaped shoreline made it a haven for people who flocked to the area in search of keepsake seashells. Strict building codes had kept high-rise developments from popping up and blocking the view. The few waterfront resorts that dotted the coast were historic Florida motels refurbished for today's savvy travelers. The lack of development kept that Old Florida feeling alive.

As they were nearing Mrs. Klein's house, Emily glanced back and forth between Anthony and the road ahead.

"What?" Anthony voiced his concern since Emily clearly had something on her mind.

"I don't think I could've survived these past few months without you. Are you having any regrets about moving back home and taking on this job?"

"Em, I wouldn't want to be anywhere else." Anthony and Emily had been best friends since high school, and he didn't hesitate for a second when she offered him the job as her head technician and hospital manager.

"It still feels strange when you call me Dr. Benton at work," she said. "We need to figure that one out."

"I'll call you Em when we're outside the hospital, but at work, it's Doc. Deal?"

"Okay, I get it. But it's still weird."

Anthony was reviewing the medical record for their appointment. "I haven't seen Mrs. Klein in years. I'm surprised our classically trained piano teacher named her dog after Elvis Presley. But then again, she did love all types of music. Do you remember the good old days of our piano recitals?"

"Remember? I still have nightmares. She was so strict. I know she was an excellent teacher, but she scared me. Still does a little."

"Em, you're a grown woman and a doctor now. You need to get over it." Emily sat up straight, pushed her shoulders back, and took a deep breath as they pulled up to Mrs. Klein's beachfront cottage.

Eliza Klein was standing at the door with Elvis by her side, waiting for their arrival. Her five-foot-tall, petite frame was in stark contrast to her oversized personal style. Thick-framed reading glasses in fire engine red framed her bright, intelligent eyes. Snowy white hair worn in a short, stylish pixie cut complemented her jumpsuit that incorporated all the colors of the rainbow.

Elvis was barking and lunging at the end of his leash, trying to convince everyone he was a guard dog. The truth was the only thing he ever guarded were his dog cookies, and his smiling face and wagging tail gave away his true disposition. Elvis was twenty pounds with a white haircoat, dark brown eyes and a tail that curled up in a C-shape. He looked like a West Highland White Terrier, but Emily could tell there was another breed thrown into the mix, since his hair was shorter and softer than a purebred Westie. One thing was certain—he was cute.

"Hey, Elvis," Anthony said as he squatted down to greet the little terrier. Elvis started dancing while wiggling his whole body. After inundating Anthony with kisses, he rolled over on his back, an obvious request for belly rubs.

"He's shameless," Mrs. Klein said while shaking her head. "Anthony Torres, is that you? I should have known. I remember how wonderful you were with the animals at the shelter." Mrs. Klein had been involved with every Coral Shores animal charity and rescue group for decades and was a recurring presence in Emily and Anthony's young lives, including volunteer work they did during their teenage years.

"Yes, Mrs. Klein. It's nice to see you again. You look well," Anthony said.

"Thank you. It's wonderful that you're back to help Emily get settled. That's a big job you have there, Dr. Benton, filling the shoes of Dr. Dinsmore."

"We miss him too, Mrs. Klein," Emily said. Dr. Dinsmore had been the original owner of the Coral Shores Veterinary Hospital, and after Emily's mother passed away, he offered to sell the hospital to Emily so he could retire. She worked summer jobs as a veterinary assistant during high school and throughout vet school, so it seemed like an ideal fit.

"Emily, I'm so sorry about your mom. She was a very special lady and a wonderful friend. You look more like her every time I see you." Mrs. Klein was smiling.

Emily said nothing in return, but nodded before reaching down to pet Elvis, using the little terrier to change the subject. It was still too hard to talk about her mom in casual conversation.

Mrs. Klein was right about Emily and her mom's similarities. They both embodied their Scottish heritage with deep red hair, fair skin, blue eyes and freckles. Emily wore her hair long and straight, whereas her mom had curls, and she was a few inches taller than her mom, but those were the only obvious differences. They were naturally beautiful women who never fussed about their appearance.

"Where are my manners? Come in. Come in," Mrs. Klein said, while gesturing for them to follow her. "We're so grateful that you could make a house call. You know, I don't drive anymore."

"We're happy to be here. So, tell us what is concerning you about Elvis?" Emily asked as she set her medical bag down in the living room. "You mentioned that he's been coughing lately."

"Yes, it started last week. I don't think he's less active than usual, but it's hard to say. He loves his daytime naps in the sun. You know I don't smoke inside my house, and I can't think of anything else that could be causing it. He's still eating like a horse."

"We'll do a complete exam on him today. Is it okay if we run blood tests to help rule out an infection?" Emily asked.

"You do whatever you think is necessary. Elvis is my entire world, and I can't have anything happen to him," she said while picking Elvis up into a lavish embrace and adorning his forehead with a kiss before passing him to Anthony. "I'm going to step outside for a smoke. I'd rather not see the blood taken, as it makes me a little squeamish."

"Sure, Mrs. Klein. We'll come get you when we're done," Anthony said to reassure her.

Elvis was an angel for his exam and his blood draw. He coughed once during his checkup, so they both heard what was worrying Mrs. Klein. Even though he was a little overweight for a five-year-old terrier, he was otherwise quite healthy. Mrs. Klein adopted Elvis from the shelter when he was a puppy, and he'd been in for his routine exams and vaccines every year since.

"What do you think?" Anthony asked as Emily removed her stethoscope.

"I'm suspicious that he may have bronchitis. It could be caused by an infection or allergies. The blood test should help us figure it out. He's up-to-date on everything else, and I didn't see any concern about his medical history in the file."

Anthony turned toward the deck to confirm that Mrs. Klein was out of earshot before whispering, "Do you think her cigarette smoke could be affecting him?"

"No way," Emily said emphatically. "Even though she is a heavy smoker, she never smoked in the house. Having kids here for piano lessons all those years made her very disciplined."

"That's true. I'll go let her know that we're done," Anthony said.

Mrs. Klein was no longer smiling, and her hands were clasped together as she walked back into the livingroom. "So, Dr. Benton. How is he?"

"Elvis looks great, but I'm worried he could have mild bronchitis. I'm going to take his blood sample back to the hospital, as it may help us figure out the best way to treat his symptoms. The results will be complete this afternoon, and I can drop his medicine off on my way home tonight."

"Oh, what a relief," she said, letting her arms drop to her sides as her entire body relaxed. "My allergies have been acting up lately too. That's probably it. We are alike, Elvis and me."

"If his cough doesn't go away, it will be important to repeat his exam and take some chest x-rays. Are you okay with that plan?" Emily asked, while making a few notes in his medical record.

"I understand. I know he will get better. Can I still take him for his beach walks? You can't imagine how much he loves them."

"Sure, but maybe keep them to short ten-minute walks until his cough resolves." Emily was fully aware they walked longer distances down the beach since she often saw them near her place.

"Doctor's orders, Elvis. No chasing the birds on the beach." He tilted his head from side to side to acknowledge he was being told an important fact. "I can always bring him home after a quick walk and finish my exercise routine without him. He won't like it, though."

"Hopefully, it's only for a few days," Emily said. "I'll call you when I'm leaving the hospital tonight."

"Thank you, Dr. Benton, and thank you, Anthony. It means so much to me you're here. Say thank you, Elvis." Elvis responded the only way he knew how—with a resounding bark.

"It was great seeing you again, Mrs. Klein," Anthony said while he and Emily packed up the medical bag, making their way toward the front door. Elvis was right on their heels, insisting on one more belly rub before they departed.

As they pulled out of the driveway, Anthony and Emily both noticed the time. They were cutting it close to get back to the hospital before their next appointment.

"She's not scary at all," Anthony said. "How old do you think she is?"

"In her late seventies, maybe eighty. Not sure. I don't know why she made me so nervous as a kid. She's a very sweet lady, and she sure loves Elvis. I always see them when I'm out walking on the beach. You wouldn't believe how fast she moves. I hope I'm that healthy at her age."

"We have a busy afternoon scheduled. I'll start Elvis's lab work right when we get back. I'm starving and assuming you're going to need nourishment before the end of the day, let's stop up ahead at Wally's Gourmet Market to grab a sandwich. It's now or never," Anthony said.

"Thanks. Good thinking."

■ ■ ■

The afternoon was a blur, as usual. Emily felt confident in her veterinary medical and surgical skills, but the added stress of running a hospital was often overwhelming. Dr. Dinsmore told her it would get easier, but she wasn't so sure. If she hadn't been able to convince Anthony to leave his veterinary job in Tampa and move back to Coral Shores, she was uncertain whether she would have made the final decision to buy the hospital. She leaned on him for support more than he knew. He was a smart, talented leader and his kind, approachable personality was an asset for building relationships with both the staff and the clients. Plus, he kept her laughing all the time.

"I have Elvis's results," Anthony said, as he handed her the report later that afternoon.

"Well, it looks like it might be allergic bronchitis after all. I'll write a prescription for an antihistamine and a cough suppressant to be dispensed, but could you write up the detailed directions for Mrs. Klein?"

"Sure. Our last appointment is here, and good news, it's a new puppy exam—a Great Pyrenes named Cloud. I thought you could use that today," Anthony said with a grin on his face.

"Thank you. You're my hero."

"Tonight, Marc and I are going to the Thirsty Pelican—that new restaurant just off the causeway. It's trivia night. Do you want to join us?"

"I'd love to, but I'm wiped out. Can I get a rain check?"

"Sure, but Marc will be disappointed. Besides enjoying your wonderful company, he wanted you along for all the science trivia questions since I've got pop culture and music covered. He's so competitive. The only prize for winning is bragging rights, but that seems to be enough."

"Tell Marc I owe him one," she said. Anthony and Marc had been together since right after Anthony moved back to Coral Shores. Emily couldn't remember ever seeing him so happy and settled.

As soon as Emily finished her last exam, she called Mrs. Klein to let her know what time she would stop by on her way home, but ended up leaving a message on the machine. Reviewing Elvis's new medicine with Mrs. Klein was important, so she did not want to leave it at the front door. Since Mrs. Klein was expecting her, Emily assumed she was out for a short walk or sitting on the back deck.

"Night, everyone, and thank you. Anthony is closing," Emily said to the staff on her way out of the hospital.

■ ■ ■

She could have driven the short distance over to Gulf Beach Road in her sleep since her house was less than a mile past Mrs. Klein's. They each owned one of the few original cottages still left in Coral Shores. Developers had bought up many of the neighboring oceanfront properties in order to build gaudy McMansions. These gigantic, cookie-cutter homes were forever changing the quaint waterfront community—and not for the better.

Emily Benton, DVM, had finished her veterinary degree and was almost through her one-year university internship when her mom got sick. She traveled back and forth from vet school at the University of Florida to her hometown of Coral Shores, on the Gulf Coast of Florida, until she finished her program.

Making the permanent decision to move into her mother's small beachfront cottage was an easy one. She wanted to care for her during the chemotherapy treatments and eventually her at-home hospice care. No matter how hard it was to see her mom struggle, she was thankful for the time they had together. Emily's brother, Duncan, lived in the next town over, but he had a young family and a demanding job as a sheriff's deputy. He visited their mother as much as possible, but he didn't have the flexibility that Emily did. They were so young when their dad passed away, and it had only been the three of them for as long as she could remember.

Living in the cottage after her mom died was a practical choice, but in reality, she was too grief-stricken and exhausted to move. Since Duncan wasn't interested in owning the cottage, they had easily sorted out the details.

Emily was still working through the painful process of clearing out her mother's things, or most of them, anyway. Strangely, she couldn't bring herself to part with any of her mom's flip-flops. Every time she started sorting through them, she'd end up sobbing. Her mom had an extensive collection of fancy and playful flip-flops, and they had always defined her casual style. Emily could picture her wearing every pair of them. Letting go of less personal items had been easier, and she took comfort in knowing the local women's shelter appreciated the donation.

As Emily pulled into Mrs. Klein's driveway, she could hear Elvis barking. It wasn't the normal, happy bark that she expected. Elvis was in distress. A sense of panic took over as she walked toward the front door. Emily knocked, but when Mrs. Klein did not answer, she started pounding on the door. Trusting her instincts that something was wrong, Emily decided not to wait any longer before trying the door handle—it was locked. What next? Elvis was becoming even more frantic, so she ran around to the beach side of the cottage, hoping that the sliding deck doors would be open.

Elvis saw her approach the deck and ran to the glass doors, barking and jumping. He was moving okay, which was reassuring since he didn't appear injured. Mrs. Klein wasn't visible on the beach or inside the living room, but seeing Elvis distraught left her with no choice but to enter the cottage. Relieved when the doors slid open, Elvis leaped into her arms as soon as she stepped inside. His heavy panting turned into a coughing attack, so Emily cradled him until it stopped.

"What's wrong, Elvis? Are you all alone?"

Elvis licked her face and then started whining and struggling to be let go. When she put him down, he ran toward the small den that was off the kitchen.

"Mrs. Klein? Are you here? It's Dr. Benton," Emily called out as she followed Elvis. The moment she walked into the den, she saw Mrs. Klein collapsed face down on the floor with Elvis lying next to her, licking her hand.

"Oh, no!" Emily's medical training kicked in as she ran to her side, gently rolling Mrs. Klein on her back so she could check her breathing while feeling for a pulse. Emily recoiled at the touch of her cold skin. The urgency to start CPR disappeared. It was clear to Emily she had been dead for a few hours. Still hoping she could be wrong; Emily's fingers were resting on her jugular vein when her own hands started to shake. This was too much to take in. Mrs. Klein had been perfectly healthy only a few hours ago. What could have happened?

Time seemed to stand still. Emily must have been in shock while she sat there holding Mrs. Klein's hand, allowing the sadness of it all to sink in. She knew there was nothing she could do to help Mrs. Klein, no matter how much she wished otherwise. Tears streamed down her face and it took Elvis pawing at her arm to bring her back to reality.

"Elvis, come here, little guy," Emily called to the terrier, trying to console him. Elvis climbed into her lap but continued to whine.

As a veterinarian, Emily had lots of experience with the loss of a pet's life, but nothing could prepare her for this moment. Saying goodbye to her mom was the hardest thing she'd ever done, and all her veterinary experience hadn't lessened that struggle. She needed to take action, and she knew exactly who to call.

CHAPTER TWO

"Duncan, I need your help," she said, relieved her brother answered on the first ring.

"What's up?" he asked.

"It's Mrs. Klein. Do you remember her—our old piano teacher? She's dead. It's so awful. Can you come right away?" Emily was doing a terrible job of hiding the panic in her voice.

"What? Where are you?"

"I'm at Mrs. Klein's house. I was dropping off some medicine for her dog, Elvis, and I found her on the floor."

"Okay, I'm leaving now. Are you sure she's dead? Did you check her pulse?"

"Duncan, I know I'm a vet, but that also means I'm a doctor. She must have died a few hours ago," Emily said with authority.

"Sure, Em. Sorry. Don't touch anything, okay. Until we can figure out what happened."

"I won't. Hurry, please."

Emily moved into the living room with Elvis, trying to soothe him, but then she felt bad about leaving Mrs. Klein alone in the den. Elvis was exhausted and curled up in her lap on the couch, but the moment he heard a car approaching, he was inconsolable—shaking and barking. It had been less than twenty minutes since she called her brother, but it felt like an eternity. A quick peek through the front curtains confirmed it was Duncan who was pulling into the driveway, followed by an ambulance with its lights flashing. Emily let out an enormous sigh of relief as she picked Elvis up and moved to open the locked front door, struggling to turn both the doorknob and the deadbolt with a squirming terrier in her arms.

"Em, are you okay?" was Deputy Duncan Benton's first question for his sister.

Emily nodded, then said, "I'm not so sure about Elvis. He seems traumatized."

The EMTs approached the front door, greeting Duncan with familiarity. "Where is she?" Duncan asked Emily.

She pointed them all in the den's direction. When Duncan returned a few minutes later, he was talking on the phone with a fellow officer.

"The EMTs confirmed she's been dead for a few hours. There's nothing they could do for her," Duncan said to Emily after finishing his call.

"I already told you that," she said, somewhat annoyed that her medical assessment was being double-checked.

"I know," he said apologetically. "They have to respond to every emergency call. The medical examiner will arrive soon. Can you tell me everything you know?"

Emily recounted the sequence of events of the day with exact timing since she'd been so concerned about being punctual for her appointment with Mrs. Klein. "It doesn't make sense. I see her exercising on the beach with Elvis all the time. She was healthy, strong and upbeat when we were here earlier."

"She is old, you know. We'll have to leave it up to the medical examiner to figure it out. Does she have family in the area?"

"None that I'm aware of. She's a widow, and her only daughter, Sarah, lives in Los Angeles. Mom told me she's an interior designer married to a Hollywood bigwig."

"Okay. We'll track her down for notification." Duncan glanced around the cottage, taking in all the details. "How did you get in here?"

"When I arrived, the front door was locked. The deadbolt was also engaged until I let you in, but the beachside patio doors were open."

While looking down at Elvis, he asked, "Will you be able to take care of her dog for a few days? At least until we can contact her family."

"Yes. Do not call Animal Control," Emily said. "And, I mean it."

"Of course, I won't. If you want to leave now, I can come by the hospital tomorrow to get your statement."

"Okay. I don't want Elvis to be here when you take Mrs. Klein away." Emily picked up the distraught terrier, squeezing him tight. "He's so upset. I can't leave him in the kennel, so I'll be taking him home with me."

"This is a lot to handle, Em. I can check on you after I finish here."

"Really, I'll be fine." Emily knew she was putting on a brave face for her brother. She was desperate to get home, curl up under the blankets, and forget today had ever happened.

"What about Bella?" he asked.

"She'll be fine. She won't be happy about it, but I can keep Elvis away from her." Bella was a twenty-pound Maine Coon cat and her mother's beloved companion that Emily had inherited along with her cottage. Bella could hold her own, despite her senior years. She was about the same size as Elvis, so he would be wise to give her a wide berth.

Emily found Elvis's leash hanging on a hook near the door and then asked, "Can I go into the kitchen? I want to find Elvis's food to take with me."

"Sure, Em," Duncan said, before reaching into his back pocket and handing her a pair of gloves. "We'll need to preserve things until the M.E. confirms that Mrs. Klein died of natural causes. It's standard protocol."

"I get it. I've already touched a bunch of surfaces in here earlier today with Anthony and then again tonight, but none in the kitchen," she said while putting on the gloves.

In the pantry, Emily found a few cans of dog food and an unopened bag of kibble. She wasn't surprised to discover that Mrs. Klein was feeding Elvis a high-end organic brand of food. She double-checked there was nothing in the fridge for the dog and couldn't help but notice the healthy groceries Mrs. Klein had on the shelves. The refrigerator was full of fresh organic smoothies, cut fruit, almond milk and prepared salads. No wonder Mrs. Klein was always so full of energy. In contrast, her fridge was filled with half-eaten takeout, expired condiments and a cheap bottle of wine—a total cliché for someone who rarely prepared a home-cooked meal.

Emily grabbed Elvis's dog bed, then said, "I've got everything I need. What's going to happen next?"

"Nothing until the medical examiner gets here and releases the body. We'll do a cursory search of the house, and then it will be sealed."

"Tomorrow is Saturday, and the hospital closes early, so come before one o'clock if you need my statement. I'll be home after that." Duncan confirmed he would be there in the morning, then gave his sister a hug.

"Okay, Elvis. It's you and me tonight," Emily said as she removed her gloves and then hooked the leash to his collar. Elvis responded by attempting to pull her back to the den and Mrs. Klein, triggering another coughing spell. "No, Elvis. You need to come with me so we can start your medicine." She gently picked up the whining little terrier and all his supplies and walked out the front door.

Emily drove home on autopilot. She was numb from the events of the day and feeling overwhelmed. As a veterinarian, she always tried to avoid attaching human emotions to her patients, but she was quite certain that Elvis was heartbroken. He barely lifted his head when she pulled into her driveway, and she had to carry him into the house.

"Bella," Emily called into the cottage. She kept Elvis on his leash since she didn't know how he would behave around cats. "Bella? Oh, there you are." Emily's enormous gray-tabby Maine Coon was curled up on the top of her custom-made cat tree that overlooked the beachside garden. After a slow, disinterested glance at the front door, Bella climbed down and walked directly over to Elvis. He looked shell-shocked. Emily couldn't tell whether it was the first time he'd seen a cat, or if it was Bella's robust size that had him confused.

"Okay, you two. Please get along." Elvis lay down beside Emily and let Bella sniff him all over. Once Bella had finished, she returned to her elevated perch, content that Elvis did not pose an imminent threat. "Crisis averted for now," she said under her breath.

Emily got a bowl of water and food for Elvis, but he wasn't interested in either, despite her attempts to hand-feed him. She resorted to using cheese to get him to take his new medicine for his bronchitis since she didn't have the heart or energy to force the pills down his throat. After feeding Bella and pouring herself an enormous glass of wine, she set Elvis's dog bed beside her feet and plopped down in front of the TV. Elvis didn't think twice before jumping on the couch and into her lap—no need for a dog bed after all. Emily was scrolling through her DVR list when she realized she didn't want to be alone.

"Hi, Em. Did you change your mind about trivia night? It's about to start," Anthony said upon answering her call.

"No, I wish. I totally forgot you were out for the night. Sorry I called. I'll see you tomorrow at work." Emily was struggling to hide her emotions from her best friend.

"Em, what's going on? You don't sound right."

"Mrs. Klein is dead," she said, blurting it out.

"What?"

"I found her when I was dropping off Elvis's medicine. I think she must have died right after we left today. It's all just sinking in."

"What happened? Where's Elvis?"

"He's sleeping on my lap. I called Duncan after I found her, so he's at the house handling everything now. I drove home before the medical examiner got there."

"We're already on our way. Do you need anything?" he asked.

"Anthony, I'll be okay. I don't want to mess up your date night."

"It's not open for debate, Em. Sit tight. We'll be right there."

Despite saying the opposite, Emily was relieved that Anthony and Marc would be with her soon. Knowing when to ask for help was not one of Emily's strengths. After her mother's death, she realized that leaning on the people around her wasn't a sign of weakness after all. It had been an important life lesson—one she was glad to have learned. It made reaching out to Anthony tonight that much easier.

• • •

Anthony tiptoed through Emily's front door, which was opposite to the way he normally entered a room. Anthony was six foot three, robust, and had a friendly, handsome baby face. He was half Cuban and half Puerto Rican, and one hundred percent of the time he wore his emotions on his sleeve. That's how Emily knew Anthony had fallen hard for Marc. She was protective of him until she'd gotten to know Marc, and then she fell in love with him, too. He was perfect for Anthony. Marc was equally tall with a lean frame, white blonde hair and blue eyes. He had a blossoming career as a structural engineer at a local consulting firm, and his calm, cool and easygoing personality balanced Anthony's more fiery and impulsive side. They were proof that opposites attract.

Emily stood up to greet them, and Anthony enveloped her in a warm hug. "Oh, Em. I'm so sorry." Emily melted in his arms, letting go of the stress she'd been holding on to, and started sobbing.

"I don't even know why I'm crying. I didn't really know her."

"But in many small ways, we've both known her our whole lives. It's still a shock. She was a kind lady, and I'm glad that I got to see her today." Anthony always knew exactly what to say, no matter the circumstance.

"Is that Elvis?" Marc asked, pointing toward the couch.

"Yeah. Hey, little buddy," Anthony said, calling out to the terrier. Elvis jumped down and ran over to him, accepting his pets and rubs, wagging his tail, and then greeted Marc similarly before returning to Anthony.

"That's the first time he's moved since I got him home. Maybe you could get him to eat his dinner?" Emily asked. "He seems to really like you."

Anthony handed a bag to Emily. "Sure, but open this first."

"My favorite—red wine." Anthony had splurged on a vintage bottle from a fancy California winery.

"I think we all need a drink tonight," Anthony said. "Here's half of my coconut shrimp platter from the restaurant, too. You need to eat something."

"Let me get you each a glass. I'm driving tonight, so I'll be your sommelier." Marc took the wine and food before moving into the kitchen.

Anthony glanced at Emily with an expression that communicated, *See, isn't he the greatest?* Emily smiled and nodded back at him. They'd always been able to communicate using only a look.

Marc and Anthony were on the edge of their seats as Emily filled them in on the details of her evening, starting from the moment she arrived at Mrs. Klein's house. Their old teacher seemed so vital and full of life only a few hours earlier, so they were struggling to process the news that she had died. It was impossible to ignore the fact that she was a heavy smoker. Maybe all those cigarettes had caught up with her in the end? Emily and Anthony finished the bottle of wine, and Emily's eyes were closing when Marc announced it was time to go. Elvis was curled up between the two men and started whining when they stood to leave.

"Call me in the morning if you need anything before work," Anthony said, while petting Elvis to console him.

"You sure you're okay on your own tonight?" Marc asked. "If you want Anthony to stay, I can run home and get his things."

Emily smiled at his kind offer. "I've got Elvis and Bella, so I'm good. Thanks, guys. I love you both."

"That's the wine talking," Anthony said to Marc with a grin. "I love you too, Em. Night."

Emily took Elvis outside for a quick potty break and made it back in time to answer a call from Duncan. He had no additional information to share about Mrs. Klein, but was relieved to find out Anthony and Marc had been there.

It was only fifteen minutes later when the vet, cat and dog were all sound asleep in Emily's bed. Even Bella had accepted the fact that Elvis wasn't leaving anytime soon, allowing him to curl up at the foot of the bed.

• • •

When morning rolled around, Emily was struggling with the fallout of her choices last night. "What was I thinking, drinking so much wine?" Emily groaned to Bella and Elvis, who were staring back at her, patiently waiting for their breakfast.

Bella enjoyed her tuna medley, but Elvis just sniffed his food, then walked over to his dog bed and lay down. He had only coughed once this morning, so the medicine was helping his symptoms. After discussing it with Anthony last night, they both agreed she should bring Elvis to work with her. She didn't want to leave him alone, plus she wasn't sure she could trust Bella and Elvis to get along unsupervised.

• • •

Emily's work day was filled with back-to-back appointments, forcing her to push through the exhaustion. Anthony set up Elvis's dog bed and food in Emily's office, and he was determined to sit with Elvis whenever he had a chance. It was late morning when Duncan showed up to get Emily's statement.

"Dr. Benton, your brother is here to see you," Abigail, the hospital receptionist, said through the office intercom.

"Send him back to my office, please," Emily replied.

"Hi, Em. Is this a good time?" Duncan asked as he approached her doorway. "The hospital seems busy right now."

"It's always like this," she said, before inviting him to sit down.

"This is Detective Mike Lane," Duncan said, introducing Emily to the tall, handsome, serious-looking man standing next to him.

"Detective?" Emily realized she said that out loud and then caught herself. "Nice to meet you." While contemplating the reason a detective would be involved in Mrs. Klein's death, Anthony came running into the treatment area of the hospital, carrying a dog that was frantically pawing at its face. Moose Englewood, a chocolate lab, had a fishing hook protruding through his upper lip.

"Emergency!"

Anthony's call for help was the catalyst for a well-executed response. The entire team jumped into action to care for Moose. An IV catheter was placed and pain medicine was administered—all under Emily's direction. Once Moose was anesthetized, Emily surgically removed the fishing hook, cleaned the injury, and placed sutures to close the wound.

"He'll definitely need antibiotics, pain meds and soft food for a few days," Emily said to her team. "I'm going to talk with Mr. Englewood, and I'll be right back. Great job today, everyone."

Moose was recovering from his procedure, but he was groggy and would need rest and close monitoring in the hospital for a couple of hours, until he was steadier on his feet. Mr. Englewood confirmed they had been fishing when Moose, who was in the mood for sushi, grabbed the fish while it was still on the line. Emily reassured him that Moose would make a full recovery.

"Is my brother still here?" Emily asked Abigail on her way back to the treatment area.

"He left about thirty minutes ago. He said it was obvious you couldn't talk right now, Dr. Benton, and asked if you could come by his office after we close today."

Emily texted her brother to confirm she would be there as soon as she finished work. Forced to play catch-up for the rest of the day, Emily appreciated her clients for being so understanding while they waited. They knew they would receive the same priority care if it was their pet having an emergency. By the time she sat down at her desk to write up the day's medical records, Anthony had been successful in getting Elvis to eat his breakfast, even though it had taken all morning. He even seemed a little perkier. That didn't help to ease her guilt after ignoring him for hours.

"I promise to take you for a walk on the beach." Emily had stopped working on her records and was sitting on the floor with Elvis.

"He'd like that," Anthony said as he walked into the office. "The last client has checked out and Abigail just locked the doors. Why don't you head home, Em? I can finish up here." Anthony picked up the stack of completed records on Emily's desk that were ready for filing and sat down.

"Thanks. I'm eager to talk with Duncan. Did you know the other guy with him today was a detective? Doesn't that seem like overkill to you?"

Anthony shrugged his shoulders. "Who knows? Maybe it's a normal procedure. Call me if you learn anything new. Marc and I can bring dinner over tonight."

Emily gathered up her belongings, including Elvis's leash. "Thanks, but I'm exhausted. It's my night to check the turtle nests on the beach, so after I'm done with that, I'm going to crash. You both were my lifesavers last night. Please thank Marc for me."

"I will. And you should know, he's planning on you being there for the next trivia night." Anthony hesitated before leaving the office. Emily could tell he was worried about her, so she forced a smile—her feeble attempt to put him at ease.

"Let's go, Elvis." Emily was trying to sound enthusiastic. "It seems we have a date with a detective and my brother, the deputy."

CHAPTER THREE

Since Emily couldn't leave Elvis in the hot car, she took a chance and brought him into the police station. He was also a first-hand witness here on official business. Nobody even seemed to notice as they waited for Duncan in the lobby.

"Hi, Em. Sorry you had to come down here today," Duncan said, while approaching his sister.

"No problem. I actually stood you up first, so it's only fair."

"That was really something, watching your team in action at the hospital. If I don't say it enough, I'm very proud of you." Emily beamed at her brother's loving support. "Okay, enough mushy stuff." Duncan motioned for Emily and Elvis to follow him into the recesses of the station.

While glancing down at the little terrier, Duncan asked, "How's Mrs. Klein's dog doing?"

"His name is Elvis, and he's a little better today. Were you able to reach her daughter, Sarah?"

After entering a small meeting room, Duncan invited Emily to sit in a chair opposite him. "We spoke with her, and she's flying in tomorrow. According to Sarah, her mom received a clean bill of health from her doctor last month. She was shocked and pretty upset about her mom's death."

"I knew it. She seemed to be fine when Anthony and I saw her yesterday," Emily said.

As Duncan finished documenting Emily's account of her interactions with Mrs. Klein for the police record, Detective Mike Lane came into the office and sat down beside her.

"Miss Benton. Sorry, Dr. Benton. Thanks for coming to the station. That was quite an impressive operation today at your hospital," he said. "Is this Elvis? Can I pet him?"

"Sure, and thanks. He's friendly." Elvis happily walked over to the detective, then rolled over for belly rubs.

"He's not very subtle, though," Detective Lane said, then smiled while obliging Elvis.

"Detective Lane, do you normally get involved in a case like this?" Emily asked.

"Call me, Mike. No, not usually, but until we can figure out why she died, it remains an open case."

Emily had a perplexed look on her face when she turned back toward her brother. "When will you know what caused her death?"

"The medical examiner completed his preliminary autopsy this morning, but additional tests are still pending. It may take a few days until we have the cause. Mrs. Klein didn't have any history of heart disease, or advanced lung disease, despite her cigarette use," Duncan said.

"No stroke or lung cancer?" she asked.

Duncan shook his head no. "They identified COPD, which her doctor confirmed. He said she'd insisted for years that it was her allergies, and not the cigarettes, causing her to need an inhaler. Her symptoms were mild, and she wasn't on any other chronic medication. Quite amazing, considering her age."

"That makes sense based on how she lived her life. She was a very energetic and positive person. You should have seen her fridge. It was full of health food," Emily added. "What's next then?"

Elvis was still enjoying Detective Lane's full attention. "The M.E. has expanded the scope of the autopsy, and we're hoping to get more information when we meet with her daughter tomorrow."

Emily turned and stared at the detective. She was processing this new information, but to be completely honest, the reason she was staring had more to do with his good looks. Detective Mike Lane was over six-feet tall, with medium brown, wavy hair and light brown eyes that Emily was sure had flecks of gold in them. His athletic frame must have been developed from a lifetime of sports, and not just from lifting weights in a gym. His chiseled jaw was the backdrop to his most attractive feature, his smile. He must have sensed her thoughts, because he returned her gaze with a charming grin.

"Detective Lane—"

"Mike."

"Okay, Mike. Do either of you know if Sarah mentioned anything about Elvis? Is she planning on taking him back to California with her?"

"No, she didn't mention him, but she'd just been informed about her mom. I did tell her the dog was safe and with his vet. Are you okay if we give her your number so she can contact you directly?" Duncan asked.

"Sure. I'll keep him with me until we can figure everything out."

"Duncan, I'm headed to a meeting. Dr. Benton, Elvis, it was nice seeing you again," Detective Lane said as he was leaving the office.

Duncan was grinning at Emily from across the desk, prompting her to ask, "What?"

"Em, I know you too well. The answer is yes, he's single."

"That's not what I was thinking," Emily said in protest before she started laughing. "Okay, maybe I was."

"He's a good guy too," Duncan said. "And he was super impressed by you at the hospital today."

Emily was quiet for a moment while thinking about Detective Lane. A long time had passed since her last date. Between caring for her mom and buying the veterinary hospital, her social life had been on hold for almost a year now.

"If you don't have any plans for the rest of the day, why don't you come over for dinner?" Duncan asked. "Jane and the kids would love to see you, and you're welcome to bring Elvis."

"Thanks, but I have to get home. I'm still a little foggy from last night with Anthony and Marc, and it's my turn to check the turtle nests. How about Sunday?" Emily asked.

"Perfect. Come over after four o'clock. Jane has been complaining that she hasn't seen you in a while, so she'll be happy. We worry about you all alone in Mom's house."

"You don't need to, you know." Emily appreciated his brotherly concern, even if it was unfounded.

"I know, but I can't help it. It's a big brother's prerogative."

"I've changed a few things in the cottage—to make it my own. At first, I felt like I was betraying Mom, but I know she'd be mad at me if I didn't move on."

"She wanted you to make it your home, Em. Not her shrine." Duncan squeezed Emily's hand for support. "If you need my help to move stuff, or to paint, you only have to ask."

"Thanks," Emily said before standing and giving him a hug. She left before she started crying. Why did she always try to act strong in front of Duncan? Maybe it was her way of protecting him from feeling responsible for her grief, too.

While driving back to the beach, Emily's stomach grumbled. It was loud enough to catch Elvis's attention based on how his ears perked up and then turned toward the source of the noise. She still didn't have any groceries at home, but at least Anthony's leftover coconut shrimp would get her through dinner. Emily knew she needed to get herself organized. After running on empty for so long, the healthy contents of Mrs. Klein's fridge had inspired her. There was a flyer she remembered shoving in her junk drawer at home. It was an advertisement for Bengle's grocer, a small, local, upscale market that was now offering delivery services. She promised herself that she would place an online order today. New beginnings.

Since it was already dinnertime when they got home, Emily fed Bella first, to make sure she knew she was still the queen of her domain, followed by Elvis. He actually ate with gusto and took his pills without issue, which allowed Emily to move outside to her beachfront deck. The unobstructed views of the ocean were medicine for the soul. Elvis joined her and sat on the edge of the deck, gazing at the beach. He appeared to be deep in thought, for a dog anyway, leaving Emily to wonder if he was remembering his life with Mrs. Klein.

"Elvis, I'll take you for a short walk in a little while, okay? Closer to sunset." He appeared to accept the commitment from Emily when he laid down for a nap.

As a member of the Coral Shores Turtle Project, Emily was one of the committed volunteers identifying and monitoring new sea turtle nests on the beach. To prevent people from accidentally damaging the fragile eggs, the nests were staked off using rope barricades. Green sea turtle eggs populated most of the nests, but a few loggerhead sea turtles also returned to Coral Shores, year after year. Emily and Anthony had been volunteers in high school, and the organization was thrilled when Emily returned home as a veterinarian. It was nice having a doctor in their ranks. Increasing sea turtle populations in the Gulf of Mexico was a source of local pride. Maybe one day they could be removed from the endangered species list.

Emily dozed on and off while sitting on the chaise lounge. It had been her mother's favorite place to rest during her illness and was now Emily's go-to spot to relax. She got up during the evening to reheat Anthony's leftovers for dinner and once it was late enough; she hooked Elvis to his leash for their walk up the beach.

"Little buddy, if you cough, we'll have to turn back," Emily said. Elvis turned and looked up at her. The stakes were high, and she could swear he understood what she was saying.

While approaching the area of the beach that was her responsibility to monitor for the Turtle Project, she realized she was nearing Mrs. Klein's house. It was almost dark, but the light of the full moon reflecting off the water created a soft back light. After she concluded the nests were quiet tonight, Elvis started whining and pulling on his leash. He knew his home was close by and was determined to get back there.

"We need to turn around now, Elvis," Emily said. He became more frantic as she tried to lead him in the opposite direction. Without warning, Elvis broke free of Emily's grasp and started sprinting toward his own house. She charged after him, calling his name, and eventually grabbed the end of his leash within a hundred yards of Mrs. Klein's cottage. The only reason she could catch him was because he started coughing.

"What were you thinking? You need to take it easy," Emily said, while consoling Elvis. "I know you want to go home, but you can't."

With Elvis occupying Emily's full attention, it wasn't until she looked up the beach toward Mrs. Klein's cottage that she noticed there was a light on inside.

"What? That's strange," Emily said. She knew that Sarah, the daughter, wouldn't be arriving until tomorrow. Plus, the light was in constant motion. It wasn't from a lamp or overhead light that was on a timer. It moved erratically, reflecting off the walls and windows. Despite the closed curtains, it was obvious to Emily that someone was using a flashlight to navigate from room to room.

"Something is off here," Emily said. She picked Elvis up and walked toward the house. Once she was up on Mrs. Klein's beachside deck, she could see the outline of a person moving inside, in the shadows. Alerted to Emily and Elvis's presence, the intruder shined the flashlight in their direction through the curtains. Elvis was barking and growling, desperate to break free of Emily's hold.

"Hey, who are you? What are you doing in there?" Emily shouted. As soon as the words came out of her mouth, a wave of panic washed over her. Had she put herself and Elvis in an unsafe predicament? The person responded by turning off the light and disappearing into the darkness. Emily grabbed her phone to call her brother.

"Duncan," Emily said, whispering so quietly only Elvis and her brother could discern what she was saying. "You need to get back over here. Now."

"What are you talking about? I can barely hear you."

"I'm at Mrs. Klein's house. Someone's broken in. I think they're gone now, but I can't tell." Her whisper now took on a sense of urgency.

"Emily, move away from the house, but stay on the phone with me. I'm on my way."

"Okay. Thanks, Duncan. I'll walk around to the road and wait for you there. Wait. I think I just heard a car pulling away."

"Please be careful."

Emily could hear Duncan gathering up his keys, and then the slamming of a door, followed by his car engine turning over. During his drive back to the beach, she gave him a run-down of what she'd seen. Emily felt safe waiting for her brother as long as she could hear his voice. The beach road was long and straight, providing her an ideal vantage point. She could see a car approaching from almost a mile away, giving her time to hide.

"Did you give the keys to the house to anyone else?" Emily asked.

"No, her house is sealed, and there's police tape across the front door. Nobody should be in there." Duncan kept Emily updated on his location as he approached the cottage so she would know it was him arriving. Recognizing his car as he made the last turn in the road, Emily felt the tension in her body release. Her legs almost buckled, but after a few deep breaths, she regained her composure. Duncan's car had only just stopped moving when he jumped out and ran over to Emily. "Are you okay?"

"I'm fine, but Elvis is freaking out. We need to stop meeting like this."

"Did you see the person or any vehicles leaving the area?" he asked.

"No, but based on the person's height, I think it was a man—he was pretty tall. I didn't see his car, but I heard one driving away before I made it to the street side of her cottage. The engine was loud, like a sports car or a truck."

"I wonder how they got in?" Duncan was inspecting the cordoned off front doorway and confirmed the police seal was intact. It didn't take long until he found a large window off Mrs. Klein's kitchen that was jimmied open.

"I'm going inside, and I'll come around to let you in through the beachside patio doors. I'd rather leave the front door untouched right now," Duncan said.

"Okay. I'll meet you around the other side." Elvis had continued to whine and wiggle in Emily's grasp, desperate to get closer to his home.

Before she entered through the patio doors, Duncan turned on all the interior and exterior lights and completed a quick search of the house. Unable to hold Elvis any longer, she had to set him down. He ran around the entire cottage, growling with his hackles up, before darting toward the den. Emily could hear him puffing and pawing at the floor, and when she caught up to him, he was lying down next to where Mrs. Klein had died. His grief was palpable. That normal, spunky, terrier energy had disappeared, and he seemed deflated. Emily could no longer hold back her tears.

"He's breaking my heart." She sat down beside Elvis, attempting to comfort him by gently petting his head. He didn't move a muscle when she touched him, and after leaning closer, she could hear his low-pitched whine, repeating over and over. Emily had no idea how to help him—a very frustrating position for a veterinarian. Nobody other than Mrs. Klein could make him feel better right now, so Emily moved to join Duncan in the main area of the cottage. "What's going on here?"

"I don't know. It's obvious that whoever was in the house was searching for something," he replied. "When we left yesterday, everything was exactly as you'd found it."

While walking around the cottage, they could see kitchen cabinets and dresser drawers sitting open, with all the contents thrown on the floor. Mrs. Klein's desk, that sat near her piano, was in disarray, with papers and files strewn all over. Emily remembered that her computer had been sitting on top of the desk yesterday, but it was now missing. In her bedroom, someone had dumped all her belongings on the bed, including the contents of her jewelry box. They even broke the box into pieces.

"If this was a robbery, why leave behind all the jewelry?" Emily asked.

"I don't know, Em. I've got to call this in. I'll be right back."

Emily's heart had been racing ever since her encounter with the intruder. The pounding in her chest had subsided, but she could still feel the adrenalin coursing through her body. As she looked around Mrs. Klein's house, she could see many obvious valuables that would have caught the eye of a semi-competent burglar. There were expensive crystal collectibles on display in the living room, and a silver tea service on her dining room hutch. Mrs. Klein's purse was sitting on a bench near her patio doors. She could tell the intruder had rifled through the contents, but her wallet was still there, laying open on the floor. Credit cards and some cash were visible in the billfold, including a few twenty-dollar bills. Not a lot of money, but a thief would have taken it all. While surveying the chaos, Duncan walked back into the cottage, still on the phone.

"Okay, Mike. I'll wait for the CSI team, and we'll see you in a few." Duncan ended his call before turning his attention back to Emily.

"What's that all about?"

"A crime scene team is on their way to process the house, and Detective Lane will be here soon."

"This robbery makes little sense," Emily said, while waving her hand at the mess inside the cottage. "There are tons of valuables in here. Why would they keep rifling through all the cupboards and drawers when they could scoop up the items sitting in plain sight?"

"Exactly. This place has been tossed. Whoever broke in was looking for something specific. Since you interrupted them in the middle of it all, it's hard to say for sure. Imagine how much more havoc they could have caused if you hadn't chased them off."

"True. Do you think it's related to Mrs. Klein's death, or is it a random robbery?" Emily asked.

"I don't know, but her cause of death will now be treated as suspicious—at least until we can work through all the details. I hope her daughter can help us out tomorrow and let us know if there's anything missing."

"Do you need me to stay until your team gets here, or can I take Elvis back to my place?"

"You can leave, but I don't want you walking alone tonight. When the techs get here, I'll drive you home."

Finding the intruder had rattled her, so Emily happily accepted his offer to escort her home. With nothing else for her to do, she walked back into the den and sat on the floor beside Elvis.

After performing another brief survey of the crime scene, Duncan joined Emily. "I'm going to be here late tonight. I'd feel better if you called Anthony to see if he can stay with you again."

Emily nodded and then texted Anthony with the grim news. Anthony was already at Emily's house by the time Duncan dropped her off. He had all the lights on and assured her the cottage was secure. Anthony had packed an overnight bag and would not let Emily send him away. With her defenses worn down, she was relieved he was staying. They ordered an excessive amount of Chinese food for delivery and distracted themselves for the rest of the night by watching sitcom reruns on TV. Emily told Anthony about everything that happened tonight, but she didn't have any answers to his questions about what it all meant. She hoped Duncan could fill in the missing pieces.

CHAPTER FOUR

When Emily woke up the next morning, Bella was in her usual place, perched on the extra pillow, but Elvis was no longer at the foot of her bed.

"Elvis." Emily whispered to avoid waking anyone.

When he didn't appear, she tiptoed into the guest bedroom and found him curled up in the bed beside Anthony. She pulled the door shut without making a sound so they could keep sleeping and sat down at the kitchen table. While waiting for the coffee to brew, Emily reflected on the string of recent events. After concluding that none of it made any sense, she took her steaming cup of strong Italian roast and moved out to the chaise lounge on her deck.

Early mornings were Emily's favorite time of the day. While her cottage's west-facing view of the ocean kept her from enjoying a direct sunrise, the soft morning glow of the tropical sky was picture perfect. It was during quiet times like this when Emily missed her mom the most. Over the past few months, these moments of reflection became less weighted in sadness, and were now filled with comforting, happy memories. Hectic days at the veterinary hospital had been a great distraction from her grief, but she knew it wasn't healthy to avoid processing her feelings. Sorting through her mother's personal items had been cathartic, and as each day passed, it was getting a little easier.

Anthony, with Elvis in tow, joined her on the deck. "Morning, Em. Coffee smells great. Is it your regular super test?"

"Always. Grab a cup and come join me. I'll take Elvis out and get his food and meds while you get settled. You two looked snuggly when I peeked in earlier."

"Elvis is the man. I think he ended up sleeping with me most of the night. No coughing either."

"Good. At least one thing is going right."

"Understatement," Anthony said, acknowledging her point with a nod before they took care of feeding Bella and Elvis, while topping off their coffee.

"Any word yet from Duncan?" Anthony asked.

"No, but I wouldn't expect any news. Who knows how late they were at Mrs. Klein's last night. I left right when Detective Lane showed up."

"Too bad, right?"

"What do you mean?" she asked.

"I mean, too bad you missed chatting with the handsome detective. Em, you're a brilliant person, but you're hopeless at picking up on dating cues." Anthony was shaking his head from side to side in defeat.

"Give me a bit of a break. It was a crime scene where someone had died." Emily reached over and cupped her hands around Elvis's ears to shield him from her words.

Anthony was pointing at the confused expression on Elvis's face. "Is that really necessary?"

"It is. You haven't seen Elvis when he's been so distraught. It's really heartbreaking."

"I'm sorry, Em. I'm not trying to give you a hard time, but I feel the need to point out the obvious. You told me the detective is single and so are you. You're both young, attractive professionals that likely spend all your free time working. Having a good-looking incentive to take a break wouldn't be such a bad idea."

Emily shot him one of her looks that didn't require any words to be spoken between the two of them. Her feelings were obvious, so Anthony dropped the subject of Emily's dating life, or lack of a dating life, for now. "What's the plan for the day?"

"No plans, really. I need groceries, so I'm going to try that online ordering system from Bengle's health food market. There are a few DIY projects I'm working on for the cottage, then I'll head over to Duncan's for an early dinner. No hospital paperwork today—I'm wiped out and need some time to recharge."

"I'm glad. You need the break. Marc and I are trying out a new stand-up paddle board yoga class this afternoon. You're welcome to join us."

"Though I'm super tempted to see you bending yourself into a pretzel on the water, I'll have to pass. That would take more energy than I have to give. I'm looking forward to seeing Jane and my niece and nephew. It's been too long since our last visit."

"They are cute kids. If Duncan shares any news about last night's break-in, promise you'll fill me in?"

"I will. Promise. Since you've come to my rescue two nights in a row, the least I can do is buy you breakfast. Your choice."

"Let's try that bakery cafe up the road, Savannah's. I hear they have this amazing açai bowl," Anthony said.

"Marc must be rubbing off on you with this new health kick. I'm loading up on healthy food later today, so I'll stick with their egg and bacon on a croissant."

"What about Elvis?"

"I think he'll be okay with Bella. She keeps her distance despite his attempts at friendship. Mrs. Klein's daughter is flying in today and I'm hoping to talk with her to find out if she's planning on taking Elvis back to California."

"I know being with family is best for Elvis, but I'll be sad to see him go. He's a great little dog." Anthony was scratching Elvis behind his ears; a favorite location second only to belly rubs.

. . .

After enjoying a relaxed breakfast together, Anthony went home to get ready for his yoga class. Emily took Elvis for a quick walk on the beach before sitting in front of her laptop to check out the Bengle's grocery website.

"Elvis, your mom is my inspiration," Emily said. "The healthy food in her fridge looked tasty, too. No more takeout dinners for me."

While she was online shopping, Duncan called to see if they could move up their dinner to a late lunch. "Mrs. Klein's daughter is meeting us at the station at four o'clock today," he said.

"Okay. I haven't heard from her yet about Elvis. Can you bring it up again when you see her?" Emily asked.

"Sure. See you soon, Em."

Right after hanging up from her brother, the phone rang again. "Is this Dr. Emily Benton?" the caller asked.

"Yes."

"Hi. My name is Sarah Klein. I understand that you've been caring for my mom's dog, Elvis."

"It's great to hear from you. Yes, Elvis is staying here at my house," Emily replied.

"Thank you so much for making sure he's okay. I'm still in shock about everything that has happened," Sarah said. It was obvious to Emily she was struggling to choke back her tears.

"I'm really sorry about your mom. She used to teach me piano as a kid. She was a very special person." Emily was unsure about what to say next.

"Thank you. I've just arrived in town, and I'm meeting the police later today. I was wondering if we could get together to talk afterwards?"

At first, Emily was surprised she would delay having a discussion about Elvis, but she knew firsthand that when you're grieving a loved one, everything can feel overwhelming.

"Sure. I'll be home by late afternoon and you're welcome to come here. My house is a mile down the beach from your mother's place. I can text you the address," Emily said.

"That would be perfect. Thank you again and I'll see you later," and then she hung up.

That's weird. Why does she need to meet in person to talk about Elvis? Maybe Sarah was only focused on seeing him since he had been so important to her mom. But if she was going to take Elvis home with her tonight, wouldn't she have said so? Emily was feeling uneasy, but there was no point in worrying about the unknown.

"Okay," she said to Elvis. "Back to grocery shopping."

It was nice having a dog in the house, but she knew Bella was out of sorts, despite her aloof persona. Emily filled her virtual grocery cart with enough food to stock her fridge and scheduled a delivery for later in the afternoon when she would be home from Duncan and Jane's. The morning had flown by when Emily realized she needed to get ready to leave.

Jane had been Duncan's college sweetheart, and they'd married shortly after Duncan graduated from the police academy. They lived in a golf course and pool community in the suburbs, perfect for a young, growing family. Their kids, Mac and Ava, were always a hoot to hang out with. Mac was seven years old and big into baseball. He collected players' cards and was a third baseman on his Little League team. Ava was five and a very creative, funny and artistic kid. She was constantly playing dress up, acting out scenes from a play or drawing pictures. Both kids had hints of the Benton red hair but were closer to strawberry blondes.

Jane was the sister Emily had always wanted. They'd been close since the moment they met and routinely spent time together without Duncan. Both their lives were quite busy right now, with the kid's activities and Emily's purchase of the veterinary hospital, so they hadn't been able to connect as often as usual. Emily was looking forward to catching up with her family.

. . .

During the quick drive over to Duncan and Jane's place, Elvis stood with his front paws on the armrest while his tail wagged back and forth. It was as if he knew he was going on a play date.

As Emily pulled into the driveway, Jane ran out to meet her.

"Yay, you're finally here." Jane said before greeting Emily with a hug. "Elvis, it's nice to meet you, too." After an exuberant introduction, she obliged Elvis when he rolled over in request of a belly rub. "Cute."

"Hi, Jane. The house looks great. You look great, too. I love your new haircut," Emily said.

"Thanks, Em. Do you have any lip gloss or mascara in your bag?"

"No. Why?"

"Sorry, I didn't know he was going to be joining us for lunch, otherwise I would have given you a heads-up."

"Who?" Emily was thoroughly confused.

"Mike Lane. Duncan told me you kind of like him and I don't blame you. He's a hunk."

Emily couldn't ignore the fact that her heart rate soared at the mention of his name. She knew it was ridiculous to be nervous about seeing him again. After all, she'd only met him on two brief occasions. Still, she wished she'd done more with her hair than just put it in a ponytail or that she wasn't wearing her lazy-day play clothes.

"This is as good as it gets. Take me or leave me," Emily said, glancing in her side-view mirror.

"You look beautiful, Em. Let's go. The kids have been asking every five minutes if you'll be here soon. They're excited about meeting Elvis, too."

After saying a quick hello to Duncan and Mike, Mac and Ava dragged Emily away so they could show her all their latest stuff, but they were most excited to play ball with Elvis. Emily couldn't remember the last time she had laughed that hard. After twenty minutes, Jane told the kids they had to give their aunt a break so she could visit with the adults. Emily promised to pick back up with their games after lunch. The kids seemed happy to continue chasing Elvis around the yard. Emily noted she hadn't heard him cough at all.

As Emily walked over to join Mike and Duncan on the back patio, they abruptly stopped talking. It was obvious they were discussing the case, but didn't want to continue in front of her. Mike stood up, offering his chair before grabbing another one nearby and sitting down beside her.

"The kids really miss you, Em. We need to get together more often," Duncan said.

"Maybe they could come over next Sunday for a beach day. Mac said his baseball season is wrapping up."

Jane, who had rejoined the group, said, "They'd love that."

"So, do you have any new information about last night's break-in?" Emily asked.

Mike glanced over at Duncan before answering, "Not really. We're still waiting for the crime scene techs to finish with the evidence they collected."

"Mike joined us for lunch today since we're both meeting with Sarah Klein at the station later this afternoon," Duncan said, then smiled. Emily knew that goofy grin on Duncan's face was meant for her, but she ignored him.

"Sarah called me today, and she's coming by my place after she finishes with the two of you. I don't know what her plans are for Elvis. I guess I'll find out soon enough."

"Elvis is great with Mac and Ava," Mike said, while watching the kids run around the yard with the little terrier. "He reminds me of a dog I had as a kid, Buster. Duncan told me you're involved in sea turtle rescue as well. It sounds quite interesting."

"Yeah, I've been involved with the local group since high school. It's amazing to be there when a turtle nest erupts and you can witness all the hatchlings make their way back to the ocean."

"I would love to see that. I grew up completely landlocked in Pennsylvania. We had lakes around, but that's so different from living by the ocean."

"I can let you know the next time a nest will be hatching and you can join me." Realizing she had inadvertently asked him on a date, Emily paused. To avoid feeling awkward about the whole thing, she downplayed her offer. "There's usually a small group of us at each event. Most of the nests hatch at night, but we've had success using new technology to make those predictions more accurate."

"Absolutely," Mike said. "That would be great. I'll give you my cell number, and please let me know the next time you're going out."

Emily could feel herself melting on the inside while Duncan sat there, smiling. Jane came over to grab her husband so he could help bring out the food for lunch, leaving Emily and Mike alone. They fell into a relaxed conversation. It was common to experience a few awkward moments when two people first meet, but not with Mike. It was as if they'd known each other for years. Emily learned he had been a rookie detective in Pittsburgh before relocating for a promotion to the Gulf Coast. He'd only been on the new job for a few months and was still unpacking boxes. Mike didn't share any personal reasons behind this big move, so she planned to get more info from Duncan later.

Elvis came over to lie down in the shade beside Emily, accepting a big bowl of fresh water and a couple of dog treats she had brought with her. Jane had prepared a tasty lunch, while Duncan grilled burgers for everyone. It wasn't long after they finished eating when Mike and Duncan announced they needed to leave for the station. Mike made sure that Emily had his phone number and made her promise to call him to see the next turtle hatch. After they left, the kids went back to playing ball with Elvis while Emily and Jane caught up over dessert.

"So, he seems like a really nice guy, Em. Duncan said he's single, new in town, and doesn't have many friends yet."

"Let's not get ahead of ourselves," Emily said. "I don't have enough time to get to the grocery store these days."

"It won't always be like that. I know it's been overwhelming the past few months, but it must be getting a little easier. Isn't it?"

"It is. Thanks to Anthony. I don't know what I would do without him."

"We should get together and go out sometime soon. I'd love to see Anthony, and I haven't met Marc yet. I really could use a night out," Jane said, then sighed.

"I know the kids are pretty busy with school and all their activities, but I think you should take me up on my offer to have them over for a beach play date next Sunday. It would give you some free time," Emily said. "Plus, I miss seeing them."

"Thanks, Em. We would all love that." Jane was watching the kids attempt to teach Elvis to roll over. "What's going to happen to Elvis?"

"I don't know. Sarah Klein is coming by my place soon, and I'm assuming she has a plan." Emily glanced down at her watch before adding, "I should head home now."

"Okay, but will you promise me one thing?"

"Maybe, it depends."

"Promise me you'll call Mike. He seems legitimately interested in the turtles and in you."

"Do you really think so? Anthony has already gotten on my case about him, too. Are you both in cahoots to set me up on a date?" Emily asked.

"No, but we should be. It'll take both of us to force you out of your comfort zone."

"Message received. I'll call him. I promise," Emily said. Jane smiled, looking like the cat that ate the canary. Convincing Emily to go on a date was no easy task.

"Mac, Ava, your aunt needs to take Elvis home for his dinner. Come, say bye," Jane called out to the kids.

"Auntie Em, can we play with Elvis this week at your house?" Ava asked.

"Elvis might go to his new home in California soon," Emily replied.

Mac's disappointment was obvious when he dropped his head and shoulders. "Aww. That's not fair. We want him to be our dog cousin."

"I'm sorry, kiddos, it's not my decision. Elvis had so much fun playing with you today. Do you both want to give him a cookie before we leave?"

"Yes!" Ava and Mac got Elvis to sit and shake a paw before inundating him with hugs and pets. The kids were masterful at stretching out their goodbyes to avoid letting Elvis go. The little terrier was in heaven, soaking up all the love and attention, including an excessive amount of belly rubs. It was hard for Emily to leave.

"Thanks, Jane. I really needed this. Let's talk in a few days about plans for next weekend," Emily said.

"Bye, Em. Be safe. I love you," Jane said, while squeezing Emily in a hug.

During the drive home, Emily ran through the myriad of scenarios that could arise from her meeting with Sarah Klein—but there was no point in speculating. She held strong convictions about her role as Elvis's advocate since he no longer had someone looking out for him. What was best for Elvis would govern any decisions that came next.

CHAPTER FIVE

Shortly after Emily got home with Elvis, she received a text from Bengle's grocery store to let her know her delivery was on its way.

"Impressive," Emily said to Bella and Elvis. Right away, she received an additional text from Anthony. He had sent her a video of Marc and himself balancing on stand-up paddle boards during their inaugural yoga class. Anthony dwarfed the size of his board, but he was amazingly nimble for a big guy. It was the second time that day she had laughed so hard.

Emily noticed the Bengle's van pull into her driveway. She was excited about having groceries in the house—it had been a while. Elvis performed his normal routine of racing to the door while barking. It was his way of telling the world he was in charge. Of course, it was all for show since he was wagging his tail the whole time. To be safe, Emily put him on a leash. As soon as she opened the door for the delivery man, Elvis's demeanor changed in an instant.

"Gggrrrrrrrrr." Elvis snarled, while baring his teeth. His hackles were standing up straight on his back, and his ears were pinned to the side of his head. He looked like an attack dog. Shocked by this aggressive posture, Emily wasn't fast enough to react before Elvis lunged at the man's pant leg, biting his ankle.

"Ouch!" shouted the delivery guy. Emily pulled Elvis away from the door as fast as she could. The man started hopping on one foot, cursing, while rubbing his injured leg.

Mortified that she, the vet, had let this happen, she said, "I'm so sorry. Are you okay?"

The delivery guy was still focusing on his leg when he angrily replied, "No! I'm not okay. Your dumb mutt bit me."

"Again, I'm very sorry. He's actually a very friendly dog. He's been through a difficult trauma recently, so he's not quite himself," Emily said, trying to explain what might have happened.

"I'll show him trauma," replied the delivery man. Elvis responded by growling and attempted to lunge at him again. Emily was quick to respond, pulling Elvis away before he could make contact. The delivery man reacted by shifting his weight in preparation to kick Elvis.

"Hey! Do not touch my dog!" Emily resorted to yelling to get his attention, before lowering her voice. "I'll put him in another room and be right back." He was still growling when Emily picked him up and closed him in her bedroom. Bella was sitting on top of her cat tree but looked like she was on the verge of bolting for the nearest hiding spot. Before walking back to the front door, Emily took a deep breath. She needed to diffuse this situation since Elvis had attacked this man. It didn't help that Elvis kept barking, and growling and scratching at the bedroom door.

"You've got a big problem here, lady. I'm going to report your attack dog to my boss. You might get boycotted," said the delivery man while pointing his finger at her threateningly.

Emily took one step back before answering. "I know this doesn't excuse his behavior, but this has never happened before. His owner died this week, and he's out of sorts."

"I don't really care. He's just a mean little dog." The delivery guy was almost sneering as he spoke.

"What's your name?" Emily asked.

"Why?"

"Please," Emily asked again.

With his lip curled, his hostility was on full display. "My friends call me Bucky. You can call me Brian."

"Okay, Brian. I can assure you this will not happen again, and he's current on all his vaccines. There's a walk-in clinic close by, and I'd be happy to pay for you to go so they can treat your injury. Could you check to see if he broke through your skin?"

"Who are you? Dr. Quinn, Medicine Woman?" Bucky asked, while challenging Emily's advice.

"No, I'm his veterinarian, and I'm used to dealing with bite wounds. I can't treat your wound—you'll need to see your doctor for that. But I can look."

"Thanks, but no thanks. Here, take your groceries so I can get outta here." Bucky was holding the bags extended in front of him.

"Sure. I'm still going to apologize to your boss and make him the same offer to pay for a doctor's visit."

"Whatever." Bucky set the groceries on the floor and turned to leave, exaggerating his limp as he walked back to the delivery van. After starting the engine, he continued to stare at Emily. She was still standing in the entryway when his driver's side door opened, putting her on alert. What was he doing? Before she could contemplate his intent, he closed the door, put the van in reverse, and was gone.

Emily picked up the bags and set them on the kitchen counter before releasing Elvis from the bedroom. He charged at the front door, growling and sniffing frantically.

"Elvis, what were you thinking?" Emily asked, still rattled from the delivery fiasco. It was a rhetorical question since he was a dog and thinking clearly wasn't part of it. Emily had read through Elvis's full medical record, and there had not been a single note about him being aggressive. She'd also seen him running off leash on the beach with Mrs. Klein, and he would always greet passersby in a friendly manner. It made little sense. What was it about Bucky that set him off?

After Emily put away her groceries, Elvis was still whining and patrolling the door. He needed her help to settle down. Hoping to diffuse whatever energy was causing his behavior, she took him for a walk on the beach. After about fifteen minutes, she could see his ears perk up again. He had a hop to his step and was wagging his tail. Since he seemed to be back to his normal self, she returned home. Sarah Klein would be coming by soon, and Emily wanted to ensure Elvis was calm before she arrived. As soon as they entered the cottage, Elvis resumed sniffing around the front door. Once he was convinced that Bucky was gone, he lay down beside Emily on the living room couch.

"That's more like it, Elvis." Even Bella sensed things were back to normal and sauntered over to her food bowls for a snack.

"Okay, no time like the present," Emily said before placing the dreaded call to the grocery store. She was forced to leave a message for Mr. Bengle, who had already left for the day. "I'm not looking forward to that conversation," Emily muttered after hanging up. She also felt obligated to disclose to Sarah Klein the details of Elvis's run-in with the delivery man. Maybe Sarah could shed some light on his behavior?

Emily thought Sarah would be contacting her any time now, so she held off preparing her dinner, despite the fridge full of tasty food. She regretted that decision when it was after seven o'clock and she was starving.

A quiet knock at the door caused Elvis to charge over as usual. Emily's frazzled nerves could not handle another incident, so she picked him up in order to have full control of the situation. She opened the door and found Sarah Klein standing in front of her, crying.

"Elvis!" Sarah said, smiling through her tears. "Look at you." Elvis tried to leap out of Emily's arms so that he could greet Sarah with a face full of wet dog kisses. Sarah hugged him tight and started sobbing. Emily put her arm around Sarah's shoulder, guiding her over to the living room, so she could sit down with Elvis and compose herself.

"I'm so sorry, Sarah. Can I get you anything?" she asked while scrambling to grab a tissue box from the hall bathroom. Emily was at a loss—she didn't know what to say or do in order to help this grieving stranger. Elvis knew what to do. He leaned into Sarah, accepting her gentle massage of his ears, kissing her hand now and then for support.

"Water would be great. Thank you." Emily dashed to the kitchen and returned with drinks for both of them.

"I didn't mean to barge in unannounced," Sarah said. "I was with the police at my mother's house and realized I'd be here as fast as I could text you about my arrival time."

"No problem. We were expecting you, and Elvis seems thrilled to see you. You've both had a very traumatic week."

Sarah was staring out the patio doors toward the ocean before saying, "Your home reminds me of my mom's place. You have the most beautiful sunsets. Have you lived here long?"

"This is, or I mean, was my mother's home. She passed away this year, too." Emily's voice drifted off at the end.

"I'm sorry, Emily. What was her name?"

"Margaret Benton, but her friends called her Maggie."

"I remember my mom talking about her. I think they'd been friends or acquaintances for a long time."

"Yes, your mom taught my brother, Duncan, and me piano lessons when we were kids. I believe you met my brother this afternoon at the police station, Deputy Duncan Benton?"

"Oh, yes. Now it makes sense. He kept asking me what my plans were for Elvis. I was wondering why he was so interested. He was very kind, though." Sarah turned her attention to Elvis and began stroking his ears.

Feeling uncertain whether she should mention she was the person who found Sarah's mom and had been there when the intruder broke into the house, Emily kept silent. Sarah must have sensed her discomfort.

"The police have filled me in on everything that's happened this week. I know that you and your technician, Anthony, were likely the last people to see my mom alive, and you've been extremely kind to care for Elvis. I also know that you've been through a lot this week, too, and I'm really sorry for whatever trauma that has caused."

"Thank you. I'm okay. My brother and Detective Mike Lane will figure out what happened. I'm confident of that," Emily said, attempting to reassure Sarah.

"I am too, but I'm worried about the resources they have available to them through the M.E.'s office and lab."

Surprised by her comment, Emily felt the need to defend her brother and the local law enforcement team. "I'm sure the medical examiner is extremely thorough."

"Oh, I didn't mean to imply that I don't think they have the knowledge. It's just that the M.E.'s lab has a backlog of forensic work, so I've hired a private pathologist to assist them. Or, I guess, they'll actually be doing their own independent investigation. I've been fortunate with my career and marriage to have the resources to hire the best, and I want some answers. I need some answers."

Emily wasn't sure how Mike and Duncan would handle that news. She would have to wait to find out.

"I assume you know my mom smoked like a chimney, despite my nagging her all my life. It was such a stark contrast to her otherwise healthy lifestyle. She was an anomaly," Sarah said, then smiled as she reflected on her mom's memory. "I gave up trying to understand it a long time ago. My mom told me her recent comprehensive physical was normal, and I double checked with the doctor today. He was as shocked as I was. That's why it's so difficult to accept that she's gone." Sarah's eyes welled up again.

"I can vouch for your mom's healthy lifestyle. I would often see her and Elvis out walking on the beach. Your mom had her fridge stocked full of organic fruits and vegetables, too. I noticed when I was packing up Elvis's food."

"Exactly. It hit me hard when your brother and the detective walked with me through mom's house just now. I had given her a few pieces of expensive jewelry that were tossed on her bed. Why would they leave them there? I'm not convinced that break-in was a straightforward robbery. Or at least that's my opinion," Sarah said.

"That's what it seemed like to me, too. I surprised them in the act, so it's hard to say what they would have taken if they had more time."

Sarah reached over to squeeze Emily's hand. "I'm not sure what it all means," she said. "Finding out if the break-in is related to my mom's death is important to me. Part of me hopes it isn't. I don't want to face the possibility that something terrible happened to her. The pathologist I've hired has a forensic technology specialist who's going to help with the investigation. The only thing that appears stolen was mom's computer. She was very tech savvy for someone her age and had been taking a bunch of classes at the senior center. She was obsessed with the concept of *the cloud* and was working to store all her photos and records in virtual space. I'm hoping there's something in those cloud files that will shed some light."

Emily knew she was avoiding getting to the pressing question at hand—Elvis. Sarah looked down at the little terrier, who was still swooning over his ear massage. "Elvis was my mom's best friend. My grief has been overwhelming, but that's no excuse for not reaching out to you sooner. I'm so sorry, Emily. I've been racking my brain trying to figure out what to do. My husband is horribly allergic to dogs, and cats too. When I return home after visiting my mom, just being in her house and picking up dog dander on my clothes would trigger him to have an asthma attack. I've asked my closest California friends if they would adopt Elvis, but nobody could make that commitment. Emily, I'm hoping that you might help me find a new home for him." Sarah started sobbing all over again, as this decision clearly tormented her. "If I could keep him with me, I would."

Emily did her best to hide her surprise since she had assumed that Sarah was going to take Elvis back to California. She resorted to her base instincts and didn't hesitate before saying, "I'll make sure Elvis finds a wonderful home. He can stay with me for as long as it takes."

Sarah placed her hand over her mouth and gasped in relief. "Emily, are you sure? I feel that it's so much to ask of you."

"Well, I need to tell you a few things about Elvis's health. Your mom called me to evaluate him for a recent cough. He's doing much better on his new medicine, and I haven't heard him cough in over a day. I still need to figure out if this will be a long-term issue before asking someone to adopt him."

"Oh, I didn't know that. We talked almost daily, so I knew you were coming over, but she didn't tell me Elvis was sick. I thought it was a routine checkup. Knowing my mom, she was likely trying to avoid thinking about it too much. Is he going to be okay?"

"Yes, I think he'll be fine. There's one more thing, though." Emily hesitated before continuing. "Elvis attacked a grocery delivery man when he arrived tonight to drop off my order. He bit his leg, and I'm not sure if he broke through the skin."

Sarah interrupted before Emily could explain. "There's no way. Elvis has never been aggressive, ever. He barks a lot, but it means nothing. He does it to show off."

"I'd agree with you if I hadn't seen it for myself. He growled and attacked this man, and it took quite a while for him to calm down. After reading his entire medical record, I didn't see a single mention of this aggressive behavior. He's always been super sweet."

"Maybe it was this guy. Did he threaten Elvis?" Sarah asked.

"No, it happened the moment he walked through the door. Elvis didn't have a chance to interact with him before he started growling," Emily said, then paused, furrowing her brows in thought.

"What?" Sarah asked.

"Well, I had ordered my groceries from a small, local market. I assume your mom might have been using the same one as there's only one organic market that delivers in this area. Your mom told me she doesn't drive anymore. Maybe it was the same delivery guy." Emily was pondering this last thought when her mind started racing. She wondered if Bucky could have interacted with Elvis before tonight.

Sarah was shaking her head in disbelief. "Well, I know Elvis. He's the most loving dog."

"He is, but he shocked me today. I'd prefer to keep Elvis here for a while longer to make sure that it doesn't happen again," Emily said.

"I'm comfortable with whatever you think is best. My mom trusted you and so do I. After talking with my husband, we decided we would like to pay for all of Elvis's medical bills for the rest of his life. That includes food and grooming, treats and whatever he needs to be happy and healthy. It's the only way I can deal with my guilt for not taking him home with me. Actually, it was my husband's idea. He feels terrible that his allergies are affecting this decision."

"Oh, that's very generous. So, you're okay if I keep Elvis with me over the next week or two before considering how to find his new home?" Emily asked.

"Sure, Emily. Whatever you decide is okay with me. If it's not too much to ask, can you keep me updated about any family that's interested in adopting him? I'll feel better knowing where he's going."

"I promise to talk to you every step along the way. Elvis is a great dog, and I'll make sure he ends up in a wonderful home."

"I don't suppose you would consider adopting him?" Sarah asked.

"I hadn't really thought about it. My cat, Bella, has been very tolerant, but I know she's not happy with Elvis in the house. She's been staying up in her cat tree most of the time. My loyalty is to her since I promised my mom that I would give her the best life," Emily said.

"I understand and respect that. You'll have to thank Bella for me, for putting up with Elvis," Sarah said, then laughed. Emily was happy to have her laughter break the mood that had been smothering the room.

"I'm flying home tomorrow. The M.E. can't release my mom's body until they determine her cause of death. That was another reason I wanted to hire a private pathologist. I don't want to delay giving her a proper burial any longer than necessary. Plus, my mom's retired lawyer friend, who has always handled her legal affairs, is out of the country right now. I was hoping to meet with him in person. It'll be a day or two before I find out if there are any special requests listed in her will. My mom never talked about these kinds of things. She always said it was too morose and promised me that her lawyer had made sure she had dotted all the i's and crossed all the t's with her estate and retirement planning."

"Is your mom going to be buried in Coral Shores?" Emily asked.

"Yes, this is her home. She's going to be laid to rest next to my dad. That's the only thing giving me any peace right now."

"I felt the same about my mom. My dad died many years ago, and it was comforting to know they would be next to each other again." Emily paused while processing her own thoughts before asking, "Where are you staying tonight? Not at your mom's house, I hope?"

"No, it was too hard being there today. Plus, it's still sealed off by the police. I'm going to have a new security system installed as soon as your brother gives me the okay. I'll be heading back to Sarasota, near Armand Circle, and then my jet departs tomorrow morning. Here are my contact numbers," Sarah said, extending her business card to Emily. "Please promise that you'll call me for anything, especially if it involves Elvis."

"I promise." Emily said. She could tell Sarah was struggling. "It sounds like you'll be back soon, and we can take Elvis for a walk on the beach. That was your mom's favorite thing to do with him."

"That sounds perfect. Thank you, Dr. Emily Benton. You're my lifesaver, or should I say, Elvis's lifesaver. I feel so much better seeing him happy in your home. I'll never be able to repay you for your kindness." Sarah stood up, giving Emily a hug before turning to Elvis. "You be brave, little man. I love you, Elvis."

Once he realized Sarah was leaving, Elvis started whining. Emily could tell she was devastated to leave him behind. To prevent him from chasing after her, Emily held him in her arms, allowing Sarah to walk out the door without looking back.

CHAPTER SIX

The events of the past week had depleted all of Emily's energy reserves. She'd been operating in survival mode for so long, her physical and emotional exhaustion had left her feeling numb. Was this her new normal? Building back a healthy, balanced life was the goal, but how?

Finding Elvis his new forever home was an extra responsibility that weighed on her. She was relieved by her decision to keep him for a while longer, to make sure his cough had resolved and he wasn't showing any signs of aggression that could affect his adoption. It bought her some time before she had to make any big decisions.

In the morning, she would be back to managing the chaos associated with owning a small animal hospital. Emily was living her dream as a veterinarian, and she knew that one day soon her learning curve would level out and she could fully enjoy her accomplishments. She wanted to make Dr. Dinsmore proud and felt she owed it to her clients and patients to offer the best care possible.

Emily didn't have the energy to make a homemade dinner at this late hour and was relieved she'd ordered a variety of organic meals from Bengle's that could be prepared with minimal effort on her part.

"Chicken Tikka Masala with a side salad for me, and dog and cat food for the two of you," Emily said to Elvis and Bella, who were sitting in front of their empty bowls, waiting patiently. "Sorry dinner is so late. Won't happen again." They appeared to accept her apology after she filled their bowls.

Emily was watching the two of them together and wondered if she should adopt Elvis. Bella was adapting better than Emily could have imagined. Maybe there was hope that given enough time, they could become friends. It was too big of a commitment to make on the spot, so she pushed those thoughts aside for now. After pouring a glass of wine and transferring her dinner to a proper china plate, Emily moved outside to savor her meal.

The brilliant sun had dropped beyond the horizon, filling the sky with streaks of orange and red that were latticed with wisps of low, tropical clouds. Emily felt a melancholy wash over her while sitting on her mom's chaise lounge, watching the day fade away. Seeing Sarah grapple with her grief tonight had amplified Emily's feelings of loss for her own mom. Sometimes it was so overwhelming she didn't know if she could breathe. As her thoughts drifted off, a sense of calm and peacefulness took over. That feeling vanished the moment someone knocked at the door.

"What now?" Emily grumbled under her breath as she struggled to get up off the lounge chair, making sure that Elvis stayed out on the deck.

"Em, it's me," Duncan shouted from the front porch. He didn't normally announce his arrival that way, so Emily figured he wanted to let her know it was safe, especially after this past week.

Emily opened the door but didn't move out of the way to let him in. "What are you doing here?"

"What? No, how are you doing, Duncan?" teased her brother.

"Sorry, it's been a tough night. Come on in." Emily motioned for Duncan to follow her outside to the deck so she could resume her position in the chair.

Duncan's expression transformed from jovial to concerned in an instant. "What happened?"

Emily filled her brother in on Elvis's attack of the delivery man and then her conversation with Sarah Klein.

"So, you're going to be keeping Elvis?" he asked.

"For now. I don't have any other options. Elvis has been through so much, and he needs someone looking out for him. Sarah was devastated she couldn't bring him home with her, but it's not her fault." Emily updated Duncan about the husband's allergies.

"Elvis, you're a lucky man," Duncan said to the little terrier. Elvis lifted his head for a second before resuming his nap on the lounge chair. "It's hard to picture him attacking anything." Duncan was gently petting his head.

"Sarah told me she's hired a private pathologist. How does that work?" Concerned she was bringing up a touchy subject, Emily distanced herself from the topic by turning away from Duncan, picking up her glass of wine and taking a sip.

"Well, it's not ideal, but it happens more than you would think. We had to smooth it over with the M.E., but the pathologist she hired is one of his old friends and at the top of their field. Once he got over the blow to his ego, he seemed happy about the help. This case is weird. There's still no cause of death, and I'm not even sure we have a crime—except the break-in, of course."

"I know you and Mike will figure it out," Emily said, reassuring her brother.

"Speaking of Mike, he was talking a lot after we left my house today about getting together with you to see the turtles. But I think it has more to do with seeing you again. Are you going to call him?"

"What is it with everyone trying to set me up these days? You, Jane, Anthony—you all act like I'm some lost cause," Emily said while making a face that was clearly intended to portray her indignation. It didn't work since she couldn't help grinning while she said it.

"Em, you know that's not the reason. We think you've been taking care of everyone but yourself lately. We only want you to be happy."

"I know. I'm just giving you a hard time. Mike seems like a great guy, and there's no denying he's smart and good looking. I'd be a fool if I didn't call him."

"Okay, I'll stay out of it from here on in." Emily gave Duncan a look that implied that she didn't believe him for one minute. "Really!" he said.

"Before I go down the rabbit hole, do you know why Mike moved here?" Emily asked. "I'm assuming he would have more career opportunities in a big city compared to Coral Shores."

"His dad died a couple of years ago, and he was helping to take care of his mom. He's an only child. Anyway, she moved to a retirement village with her sister in Florida. I'm assuming there was nothing else keeping him in Pennsylvania, plus he could be closer to his mom here. I think she's in the Orlando area."

"That makes sense. No divorce or broken engagement I should know about?" Emily asked.

"No, don't think so. You know guys—we don't talk about that stuff."

She dropped the subject of Mike and got up to walk through the house with Duncan to show him her plans for redecorating her home. It was still strange to think of it as her home and not her mom's. Her ideas were mostly cosmetic involving paint and furniture, but a few would require a contractor. Duncan was fully supportive and committed to help her as much as he could. After saying hi to Bella, Duncan left for home, but not until finalizing the plans for Mac and Ava to spend next Sunday with Emily at the beach.

. . .

On Monday morning, Emily woke up a little more energized than she'd been feeling in months. Maybe it was the result of eating a healthy, balanced dinner last night. Astounding how that nutrition thing works.

Elvis came with her to work and seemed to relish his new celebrity status. He loved hanging out in her office, soaking up all the attention from the staff. She didn't see any signs of aggression from Elvis. He loved everybody. Even better, he had only coughed once in the past couple of days. He was exerting himself chasing sandpipers along the shoreline, but this time, a solitary cough didn't turn in to a coughing attack. Emily considered that progress.

By early afternoon, Emily was still waiting to hear from Mr. Bengle, of Bengle's Grocer, so she called to follow up. She didn't want Bucky, the delivery guy, ignoring a bite wound until it became a festering problem. Bite wounds almost always turn in to a serious infection if not treated promptly with antibiotics and wound care. She didn't know if Elvis had broken through his skin, but didn't want to take a chance. *No news was good news* didn't apply in this situation. Mr. Bengle was out for most of the day, but would be back in the store by late afternoon. Emily told the person on the phone she would stop by this evening to talk with him in person and would appreciate it if they would let him know.

Emily filled Anthony in on Elvis, the attack dog from last night. His response was the same as everyone else's—pure disbelief.

Before closing time, Anthony came into the office, "Em, I think I should come with you tonight to Bengle's. Hear me out. You can't leave Elvis in the car while you're inside, and it's out of the way to drop him off at home before your meeting. I can keep Elvis on-leash in the parking lot in case Mr. Bengle wants to meet Elvis for himself. He'll see how friendly he is, and maybe it will diffuse the situation." Anthony's points made perfect sense, and Emily was happy to accept his help.

"I printed up his vaccine report to show Mr. Bengle that he's current with his rabies. Don't let me forget it, please," Emily said.

Anthony gave her a thumbs up before walking to the lobby to greet her last appointment.

Throughout the day, the Coral Shores Veterinary Hospital operated like a well-oiled machine. *Maybe Dr. Dinsmore was right,* Emily thought. It does get easier. There were a series of routine medical appointments; ear infection, skin infection, bee sting, a post-surgical follow-up for a dog that had eaten a corn cob the previous week resulting in emergency surgery, and a couple of annual routine checkups with vaccines. Emily kept waiting for the other shoe to drop, but it didn't. The staff could get home on time tonight—a rare occurrence.

"Thank you, everyone, for all your hard work," Emily said to her team. "Today ran as smoothly as I can remember, and that's a result of all your efforts behind the scenes. The strategic changes we've been making to streamline hospital operations are really paying off." Her team gave themselves a round of applause and high fives.

"Bagels and cream cheese on me tomorrow morning," Emily said, which was met with an affirmative shout-out from her staff. Success felt good, and Emily was fortunate to have a wonderful, talented and caring team to lead.

Anthony was grinning while waiting for Emily back in her office.

"What now?" she asked.

"I'm proud of you, Em," Anthony said. "In case you don't know it, the staff are very happy. They love working here and really believe in you. I've worked in a lot of different veterinary hospitals, but none that were as committed as this group. That's because of you."

"Thanks. I really needed to hear that, but I think you have just as much to do with our success. My head has been stuck in the sand lately, and if I don't say it enough, I want everyone to know how much I appreciate them." Emily looked out into the treatment area of the hospital, reflecting on their achievements.

"They know." He grabbed Elvis's leash and vaccine records, and the three of them drove over to Bengle's.

. . .

It was a busy time at the grocery store. People were making last-minute stops on their way home from work to pick up one of the delicious prepared meals from the hot and cold food bar. Anthony had planned to walk Elvis around the periphery of the parking lot so he could stay on the grass, avoiding the hot pavement, while Emily went inside. Mr. Bengle could see her right away, and a staff member showed her into a back office near the receiving doors.

"Thank you for meeting with me today," Emily said, and then smiled. Mr. Bengle was a short, stout, older man and his kind face immediately put her at ease.

"So, I understand there was an issue during your grocery delivery last night." Mr. Bengle cleared a place for them to sit. "Can you tell me what happened, please?"

Emily ran through the details of the encounter before presenting Mr. Bengle with a copy of Elvis's vaccine record. She reconfirmed her offer to pay for Bucky, aka Brian, to get a medical checkup.

"Elvis is with my friend in the parking lot, in case you want to meet him."

He took a moment to look at the records before asking, "Can you assure me your dog will be secured in another room during future deliveries?"

"Absolutely. I guarantee this will never happen again. I know you can only take my word for it, but Elvis is the sweetest dog."

"That's good enough for me, Dr. Benton. You came in today, and I appreciate that. Don't worry another minute about Bucky. When he was limping around this morning, trying to get off work early because of this alleged bite wound, I made him show me his leg. There's not even a scratch." Emily let out an audible sigh of relief.

"I appreciate your business, and as long as you can make sure that future deliveries happen without another incident, let's call this case closed. Okay?" Mr. Bengle asked, with his hand extended.

"Thank you, Mr. Bengle," Emily said, while vigorously shaking his hand. "Thank you so much. Your online delivery service was so impressive. I thought you were going to boycott me after last night." Mr. Bengle laughed before reassuring her that would never happen. They walked together to the front of the store before he thanked her again for her honesty.

Emily was all smiles as she left Bengle's, scanning the parking lot for Anthony and Elvis. As soon as she saw the expression on Anthony's face, her smile disappeared. He was kneeling down beside Elvis, working hard to calm him. Emily sprinted over to them as fast as possible.

"What's wrong? Are you okay?" Emily was running her hands all over Elvis to check for injuries.

"Let's get out of here," Anthony said while looking over his shoulder toward the back of the store. "Can you pull the car over? I'll fill you in after we leave."

It was hard to remember the last time she had seen Anthony this upset. To top it off, Elvis's behavior was identical to last night. He was panting and trembling, with his hackles standing straight up. Anthony sat in the back seat beside Elvis, attempting to reassure him so he would calm down.

"What happened?" Emily asked.

"I wouldn't believe it was possible except I witnessed it for myself," Anthony said. "By any chance, was this delivery guy from last night tall and muscular, in his mid-twenties, brown hair to his neckline and cut sort of like a mini-mullet?"

"That sounds like Bucky. Why?" Emily answered, feeling anxious about what was coming next.

"Well, I was walking Elvis around the back of the grocery store, trying to find some shade. A Bengle's delivery van pulled up to the loading doors and this Bucky guy gets out. It took less than five seconds for Elvis to zero in on him. He started growling and lunging on his leash, trying to charge toward the guy. He wasn't the same dog. It wasn't easy, but I picked Elvis up and turned my back to Bucky. I don't think he realized what was going on. He might have glanced in our direction, but then went in the back door of the store. I've been trying to calm Elvis down ever since," Anthony said.

Emily couldn't believe it. She'd just reassured Mr. Bengle that nothing like this would ever happen again, and right as those words were coming out of her mouth, Elvis was trying to attack Bucky. She couldn't make sense of it. Charging at her cottage door when a stranger approached was easier to rationalize, but acting the same way in a neutral place was too much of a coincidence. Elvis detested Bucky, but why?

"Em, don't worry about taking me to my car at the hospital," Anthony said. "I'll stay here with Elvis until we get back to your place."

Only ten minutes later, they were pulling into her driveway. Getting Elvis settled at home was easier than expected when he became distracted by Bella and his dinner, allowing Emily and Anthony to take a collective deep breath.

"What the hell is up with Elvis?" Anthony asked. "That was the craziest thing I've ever seen. He could have attacked him."

"I don't know, but it means something. Last night, I wondered if Elvis had previous interactions with Bucky. If he was the same person who made grocery deliveries at Mrs. Klein's house, maybe something happened during one of those deliveries?"

"Elvis was walking around the parking lot and lifted his nose, like he caught a scent, and that's when he turned and started growling. He didn't see Bucky at first; he smelled him."

"Well, we know terriers are famous for their sense of smell. It might be how he remembers him," Emily said.

"Probably, but it was shocking how fast his demeanor changed. It was instantaneous." Anthony had followed Bella to her cat tree and was petting her under her chin, a favorite spot. The resulting purring sounds that echoed throughout the cottage were a wonderful antidote for their anxious energy.

"That's what happened last night. There was no time to react. I need to be diligent and keep Elvis away from the door if I order from Bengle's again. This makes me uneasy, but I don't think Elvis is a risk to anyone else. There's something about this Bucky guy. There's a chance we'll never figure it out."

Anthony agreed with a nod. "If you're okay, I'm going to head home."

"Sure. Let me order you a lift back to the hospital," Emily said as she pulled Anthony's ride up on her app. "Thanks again for coming with me."

"No problem. Marc wanted me to let you know he's expecting you to join us for trivia night this Thursday. He's cashing in on that rain check."

Emily laughed. "Jane and I were talking about getting together for a night out, and she mentioned she hadn't seen you in a while, and still hasn't met Marc. I'll confirm with her, but let's plan on the five of us going, assuming Duncan can get off."

"Done. I'll make the reservations for eight o'clock, so we have time to decompress after work." It was only ten minutes later when Anthony's ride showed up. "Night, Em. See you tomorrow."

Emily realized this was the first fun social event she'd planned since her mom died. She'd been living in a fog. Taking steps to restore some balance in her life felt good, even if it was a simple dinner out with friends.

CHAPTER SEVEN

The next few days at work were downright boring compared to the previous week, and Emily was okay with that. She'd experienced enough recent excitement to last the year. Elvis was adjusting well to his new life. He loved coming with Emily to work and had appointed himself the official mascot of the Coral Shores Veterinary Hospital. After venturing out of Emily's office, Elvis spent some time in the hospital's front entrance with the receptionist, Abigail, greeting customers from his dog bed that sat on a chair beside her desk.

He had recovered enough of his mojo that he'd even tried to entice Bella to play with him. He would bow down, inviting her to chase him, and then bark and spin. Bella watched his less than civilized attempts at friendship and would turn and walk away, escaping to one of her many cherished, elevated perches. It didn't seem to deter Elvis as he pulled out all the stops in his attempts to impress her.

The Coral Shores Turtle Project was expecting a few nests to hatch any day now, so Emily had been taking nightly walks up the beach to monitor them. Elvis insisted on accompanying her, and Emily was happy to report she hadn't heard him cough in days. She always felt anxious as they approached the turnaround point on the beach, which was within view of Mrs. Klein's cottage. They had to get close in order to confirm there were no signs of trouble, which caused Elvis to pull at the end of his leash. He wanted Emily to follow him to the only home he'd ever known. Each night, it was becoming a little easier to coax him to turn around. She was often overcome with a moment of sadness while reflecting on Mrs. Klein's death until Elvis's antics on the beach would distract her with laughter.

Neither Duncan nor Sarah Klein had shared any new information about the status of the investigation, and Emily was wondering if they were doing it on purpose. Since she had been central to all aspects of the case, didn't they owe it to her to keep her informed? Emily decided she would reach out to Sarah Klein when she returned home, under the guise of sharing a glowing update about Elvis. Maybe she could also pick up a few investigatory details.

. . .

"Hi, Sarah."

"Emily, how are you? Is everything okay with Elvis?"

"He's doing great. His cough seems to have cleared up, so I'm going to wean him off his medicine starting tomorrow. He's become quite a celebrity at the hospital. All the staff and clients look forward to seeing him every day."

"That's the Elvis I know. Does that mean you're ready to find him a new family?"

"Not yet. He's been wonderful, but I still want to make sure his cough doesn't return," Emily said. She decided against telling Sarah about the recent incident at Bengle's grocery store. There was no point in upsetting her when Emily still didn't understand what it all meant.

"I'll admit that I'm relieved he's still with you. My heart breaks when I think about him going to a new home. I know whoever you pick will be wonderful, but I can't help myself," Sarah said, her voice cracking as she finished.

Emily was not looking forward to that day either, so she pushed away those thoughts for now.

"I also wanted to check in to see how you're feeling." Emily said. While she was tempted to ask if there was any news about Sarah's mom, she decided at the last minute to wait and see if Sarah would volunteer some information on her own.

"To be honest, I'm really struggling. I will not get any closure until I can give my mom a proper burial. All her friends and former students are constantly asking me when her funeral will be," Sarah said. "I'm hoping to hear from my pathologist tomorrow with the results of some tests that are pending."

"Oh, so they still don't know what caused her death?" Emily immediately regretted probing for details.

"No, not yet."

"I wish there was something I could do." Feeling both helpless and frustrated, she said, "I've been checking on your mom's house every day, and it seems secure. I've seen no one around."

"Thanks, Emily. I feel better knowing you're keeping watch. I think until I can get some answers, there's nothing we can do."

After promising to call with regular updates about Elvis, she could tell that Sarah appreciated being included in his care. Emily was left with an uneasy feeling since it appeared nothing had progressed with the investigation.

. . .

It was trivia night at The Thirsty Pelican. Anthony had been building up the event all week, and his enthusiasm was infectious. Emily was giddy with excitement, thinking ahead to her night out on the town. For months now, she'd been home alone with her own thoughts and way too many frozen dinners. Sitting in the middle of a bustling restaurant was going to result in a bit of culture shock at first, but her mouth had been watering ever since Anthony told her the restaurant was famous for their mango daiquiris and shrimp tacos.

Bella and Elvis had proven they could be left alone without incident, so Emily planned to take a ride share to the restaurant. She wanted to enjoy her night without worrying about driving home. Duncan was going to be there with Jane, and it was Emily's plan to hit him up for some information about the case after he had a couple of drinks. Maybe it would work? Duncan could be stubborn sometimes, so in the end, a drink or two wouldn't likely make a difference. He'd either tell her or he wouldn't, regardless of her master plan.

"Mr. Englewood is coming in with Moose to recheck his lip incision," Anthony said. "It's our last appointment of the night, so fingers crossed we get out on time."

"Great. I'd like to walk Elvis on the beach before leaving for the restaurant. I figure if he's worn out, he'll be more apt to leave Bella in peace. Plus, I need to do a quick check on the turtle nests before dinner."

"What are you wearing tonight?" Anthony asked.

Emily raised her brows and had a curious look on her face. "I don't know? Shorts, t-shirt, flip-flops. Why?" she answered cautiously.

"Well, you haven't been out in a long time, so I thought you might like to dress up."

"This is south Florida. Nobody dresses up. I thought the Thirsty Pelican was a casual waterfront place."

"It is. You're right. I'm so happy you're coming tonight. I think it'll be good for you."

"Me, too."

As expected, Moose's recheck appointment was routine. His lip was healing nicely, and Mr. Englewood assured her he would be more careful with Moose when they were out fishing. Emily rushed to wrap up her day, allowing the staff to leave together and on time.

. . .

"Sorry, Elvis—only a quick walk tonight. We don't have time to be chasing crabs or sandpipers," Emily said as they pulled in to her driveway. After saying a brief hello to Bella, Emily hustled Elvis along the beach. As they approached the turtle nests, she could see two of the lead turtle volunteers were already on site.

"Hi, Emily. Who's your friend?" Marlon, the president of the Turtle Project, asked.

"This is Elvis. He's friendly, but I'll keep him over here so he doesn't accidentally disrupt the nest."

"Hey, little guy." Marlon was obviously a dog person and kneeled down to pet him. "Did you say his name was Elvis? He looks a lot like Eliza's dog."

"Actually, he is or was, I guess. I'm taking care of him for now," Emily said.

Marlon looked up at Emily and smiled. He'd known Eliza Klein for decades and Elvis was her pride and joy. "I still can't quite believe she's gone," he said.

Emily nodded but stayed silent. As far as the public was concerned, Eliza Klein had died from natural causes. It wasn't Emily's place to contradict him. That piece of information would have to come from the police.

"So, do you think these nests will hatch tonight?" Emily asked to change the subject.

"Tonight, or tomorrow night, is my best guess. We came early to make sure there weren't any large hills or holes or debris on the beach between the nests and the ocean," Marlon replied as their colleague, Sharon, joined the group and heaped more attention on Elvis. They all knew that any small physical obstruction could affect the hatchlings' success of making it safely to the ocean.

"Will you both be here all night?" Emily asked. "I have plans to go out, but I can cancel them if you need my help."

Both Marlon and Sharon were well aware of the stress Emily had been under this past year with her mom's illness and the purchase of the hospital. They were also clients of the Coral Shores Veterinary Hospital and had recently been in with their furry family members for checkups.

"Thanks, Emily. We're okay, but we can let you know if we see signs of a hatching—in case you can make it back in time."

"Thank you. That's perfect. I can cover tomorrow night if needed."

Emily said her goodbyes and hurried home with Elvis. After a quick shower, she had less than thirty minutes to get ready before leaving for The Thirsty Pelican. Emily was wearing a pair of her mother's favorite flip-flops tonight, a navy-blue pair with a single crystal stone on the strap. She had incorporated her mom's sandals into her own wardrobe, and every time she put on a pair, she felt connected to a warm memory of her mom. It was a silly thing, but it made Emily happy to wear them. Her phone app dinged to let her know her ride was a minute away. As she looked around to ensure everything was secure at home before locking up, Emily saw Bella staring at her from her cat tree. She'd been neglecting Bella and committed to make time to play with her and brush her out.

The Thirsty Pelican was hopping. Emily loved that familiar crunching sound coming from the car tires as they drove across the seashell-surfaced parking lot. The weathered-gray building had striped blue awnings over the entry porch and a six-foot tall wood cutout of a jovial pelican, raising his beer stein in a toast. It appeared to be a perfect spot for selfies. It took Emily a minute to scan the crowd before she saw Marc and Anthony sitting at a high-top table in the bar area that overlooked the dining room and outdoor waterfront tables. The entire restaurant offered an expansive view of the crystal blue water that extended from the inland causeway to the open water of the Gulf.

"This place is amazing. I can't believe I didn't know about it." Emily said, while greeting them each with a hug.

"It's been open for a while, Em, but I don't think you've exactly been in the bar scene frame of mind lately," Anthony replied.

"True. How are you doing, Marc? I've been meaning to thank you for helping me out the other night. I was such a mess."

"You handled that better than I would've, that's for sure," Marc said, smiling.

"Here. We ordered you a mango daiquiri," Anthony said while moving the cocktail in front of Emily.

She took one sip, closed her eyes, and sighed. "Heavenly."

It wasn't long before Duncan and Jane joined the group. They hit it off right away with Marc, but Emily already knew they would. The first competition round of trivia night was starting soon, and their entry box was sitting in the middle of the table—ready to go. TVs lined the bar area to display each of the questions. After a quick strategy session, they agreed to play as one team. Strength in numbers.

Emily noticed Duncan waving at someone behind her, toward the entry area of the restaurant, but it didn't register until she looked over at Jane and Anthony. They both had huge smiles plastered across their faces. As soon as Emily turned to see who it was, she knew why. Mike Lane was making his way through the crowded restaurant. Emily's heart started racing, and she realized she was holding her breath. Now it made sense why Anthony had been asking her if she was going to dress up tonight. He and Jane had been conspiring behind her back.

"Hey, Mike. Glad you could make it," Duncan said, while pulling over another bar stool, which he placed beside Emily. "Great timing. We're about to start the game. Mike, this is Anthony and his partner, Marc."

"Nice to meet you all," Mike replied. "Thanks for inviting me. This place is great."

Emily still had said nothing, but was regaining her composure. Mike Lane could take her breath away. Just then, their waitress came by, so they ordered another round of mango daiquiris.

"One light beer for me," Mike said. "I'm driving."

Trivia night started right after they'd ordered their food, and that distraction helped Emily rid herself of the nervous butterflies that had been sitting in the pit of her stomach since Mike walked in. The game was a blast. Each of them contributed a unique niche of expertise, and after round one, they were in first place by a few points. Emily had the final say on all science questions. Jane had geography and current events, Duncan and Mike covered sports, Marc was a history buff, and Anthony was the lead expert on anything to do with music and pop culture.

Now and then Emily's arm would brush close to Mike's, and she could feel the electricity between them. She didn't think she was imagining it when she caught Mike looking at her out of the corner of his eye. Anthony was trying to act nonchalant all evening, but he kept close watch on every one of Emily's and Mike's interactions. Her mom would have called him a *Nosy Parker* for spying.

After they'd finished round two of the trivia contest, Emily got a text. Marlon and Sharon had sent out an update that two turtle nests were showing signs they were about to hatch. If Emily wanted to see the hatchlings make their way to the ocean, she would have to leave right away. What terrible timing. She was having so much fun and still hadn't found the right moment to question Duncan about the case. It was a trade-off she was willing to make, plus she felt an obligation to help.

"I'm sorry, everyone, but I've got to go," Emily said as she stood up and grabbed her purse. "The turtles are hatching, and I need to get back to the beach."

"Can't you stay until the last round of questions?" Anthony asked. Emily could see the disappointed look on Marc's face. He really wanted to win tonight.

"Sorry, no. But this was a blast. Let's promise to do it again real soon," Emily replied, while looking through her purse for her car keys. "Oh, I forgot. I didn't drive tonight."

Mike Lane had a huge smile on his face when he stood up. "Perfect. I can drive. You promised to include me the next time so I could see a hatching. How about now?"

Emily's surprise kept her from replying right away. Anthony was looking at her while nodding in Mike's direction, desperate to get her to snap out of it. He clearly couldn't take it any longer when he spoke on her behalf. "Emily would love to show you the turtle nests. It's really a once in a lifetime event."

Finally able to compose herself, she said, "Yes, thanks, Mike. That would be great. Anyone else want to join us?"

All four of her remaining teammates politely declined, citing various reasons, including the fact that none of them had driven their own cars to the restaurant. Plus, there was no way they were going to interfere with a potential first date.

"Okay, then. Let's go, Mike. We can park at my place, so I can let Elvis out before we walk up the beach."

Mike was grinning all the way to the car. Emily tried to play it cool on their drive to her cottage, giving Mike some information about what to expect at the hatching. He couldn't hide his childlike excitement about seeing the turtles. It was a contrast to his serious detective face that Emily had experienced during their first few meetings.

After arriving back at Emily's place, they took a few minutes to give both Elvis and Bella some attention, including a few treats. Emily knew they had to hurry to avoid missing the main event. Elvis was not happy about being left behind, but Emily couldn't have him disrupting the turtles tonight.

As they approached the nests, there was a small group of regulars that had shown up for the event. Most of them were turtle project volunteers, committed to ensuring a successful hatch. Emily introduced Mike to her friends and noticed Sharon giving Marlon an elbow in the ribs as they whispered about Emily's handsome date.

No matter how many times she witnessed this incredible feat of nature, Emily was always in awe when the turtle hatchlings emerged from their nests to start their treacherous journey to the ocean. The sand looked like it was boiling right before the hatchlings appeared.

Mike was captivated by the entire process. He and Marlon had become fast friends, as Marlon was very generous with his time and knowledge, answering an unending number of Mike's questions. His interest in the experience was genuine and when a new nest hatched, he involuntarily grabbed Emily's hand, bonding over their shared experience. The gesture felt natural, and Emily enjoyed having her hand enveloped by his large, strong grip. For those few minutes until they released their hold, Emily was oblivious to the turtles. It might have been the lingering buzz from her mango daiquiri or the woozy feeling from the butterflies in her stomach, but she felt very attracted to Mike. It'd been so long since she felt this way about anyone—the feelings were both strange and wonderful.

Once the volunteers were confident all the hatchlings were safely back to sea, the group broke up, all headed in different directions. Emily and Mike turned to walk back to her cottage.

"Thank you, Emily," Mike said, taking her hand in his as they walked along the waterline. He turned and smiled at Emily when she gently squeezed his hand in return, leaving no doubt that his gesture was welcome.

"I'm glad you could be here tonight. I try not to take it for granted, but seeing it through your eyes reminds me of how lucky I am to have grown up in Coral Shores."

"Marlon was trying to enlist me as one of his volunteers," Mike said. "I'm not sure I can commit to a regular schedule with my job, but could you keep me posted on any future hatchings? I'd love to see that again."

"Sure, and I'll get Marlon to add you to the list."

They walked the rest of the way home in relaxed conversation about Coral Shores and the beach community. Mike had rented a furnished apartment when he moved to town until he could figure out exactly where he wanted to live. The more Emily told him about her beach lifestyle, the more interested he became to check out the local real estate listings.

"This is my place," Emily said, pointing to her cottage. "Do you want to come in for a drink?"

"Sure. That would be great."

Elvis was waiting for them as they came through the patio deck. He quickly forgave them for leaving him behind after getting a few cookies and belly rubs.

"Duncan told me this was your mom's house."

"Yeah, I've started trying to make it mine, but it still feels like her home. In a good way, you know."

Mike nodded while walking around the living room. He was looking at all the family pictures and taking in the warm comfort of the space.

"What would you like to drink?" Emily asked.

"Do you have any light beer?"

After pouring herself a glass of wine, she handed Mike a bottle. "Let's sit outside," she suggested.

Elvis followed the two of them onto the deck and before she could say anything, Mike sat down in Emily's mom's chaise lounge. At first, she felt protective of her special space but caught herself, recovered, and grabbed a nearby chair.

"This is so comfy," Mike said. "How do you ever pull yourself away from here?"

"It's hard sometimes, especially this past year." Emily thought her mom would get a kick out of the fact that Mike had settled into her chair, unaware of its significance. She'd be happy for Emily.

"New hospital for you, new city and job for me. It can be a lot sometimes."

"That was a big move from Pennsylvania to Florida. Any regrets?" Emily asked.

"None. I was ready for a change. A big change."

Emily wondered if there was a story behind his answer, but she decided to tread lightly for now. Good fortune had brought Mike Lane into her life, and she didn't want to push too hard while they were getting to know each other. Mike was close to finishing his beer, so Emily took a chance and forged ahead with the questions she had planned for Duncan tonight.

"I spoke with Sarah Klein yesterday," Emily said. Mike raised his eyebrows, but he said nothing. "I was calling to give her an update on Elvis."

"I'm sure she's indebted to you for taking him in." Mike said, then smiled down at the terrier, who had curled up for a nap.

"She is. She also mentioned she was eager to plan her mom's funeral. I know she can't do that until the medical examiner releases her body. Is that right?"

"Yes, that's true." Mike said.

He was clearly unwilling to talk about the case, but that didn't stop Emily from pushing on. "Sarah was hoping to hear from her private pathologist about some test results. Do you know if they're back from the lab yet?"

"Emily, you know I can't discuss this. Not while it's still an open investigation."

"Understood, but doesn't my status as a two-time eyewitness change things? Even Marlon and Sharon still think Mrs. Klein died of natural causes, and I promise not to share any details about what's happened."

"What about Anthony?"

"Anthony is family, so he doesn't count. Plus, he's also been indirectly involved."

Mike was quiet for a minute. He finished his beer and then stood up from the lounge chair. Emily knew she'd pushed too hard and right away regretted her line of questioning. Walking over to her chair, he put her at ease when he grabbed her hands, inviting her to stand.

"I had a great time tonight. It's the first moment I've felt a strong connection to this place since moving here. Thank you for that," Mike said.

Emily smiled. "I think we all needed a night out. At least, I know I did."

"I have an early start tomorrow, but I was wondering if you would like to go out for dinner this weekend? Saturday?" he asked before melting her with his hundred-watt smile.

"I'd love that," Emily replied, maybe a little too eagerly.

"Great. I'll call you tomorrow and we can make plans." Once again, Emily found herself speechless and replied with a nod.

Mike started toward the front door, still holding her hand, but before leaving, he turned to face her. "Thank you for bringing me to the turtle hatching tonight. Easily one of the coolest experiences of my life."

"You're welcome. Anytime," Emily replied and before she could say anything else, Mike leaned down and gave her a gentle, lingering kiss goodnight. What else could she say? Emily was still standing in the doorway as Detective Mike Lane pulled out of her driveway.

CHAPTER EIGHT

Emily woke up on cloud nine, still in a haze after last night's kiss. She set her coffee on the deck and went back inside to gather Bella. Lifting her twenty-pound Maine Coon cat took both hands as she carried her out to the chaise lounge. Bella loved to be brushed while sitting in the warm sun and relished her mom's special chair as much as everyone else did. When her mom was sick, Bella had spent many hours curled up beside her, playing her part as an emotional support cat. Bella was purring while Emily daydreamed.

"Bella, I have to go to work, but I promise to brush you when I get home."

Emily loaded Elvis into the car and was driving along Gulf Beach Road when she noticed a few cars parked in front of Mrs. Klein's house. They appeared to be official cars from the Sheriff's office. Emily parked across the street while trying to figure out what was going on. She didn't see either Mike or Duncan's vehicles, only crime scene vans. There were a few people in uniform carrying large paper bags out of the house, placing them in their lab vans.

Elvis had his paws up on the window and whined while watching the commotion. He knew it was his house. Instead of asking the crime techs about what they were doing, Emily went right to the source. Unfortunately, Duncan's phone went straight to voice mail.

"Duncan, it's Em. I'm sitting across the street from Mrs. Klein's house, and there are crime scene techs carting a bunch of stuff out of her place. What's going on? Call me as soon as you get this message. Please."

Emily wondered if she should wait to hear from Duncan before leaving, but she knew it could be a while, plus she had to get to work. If she waited any longer, Elvis would work himself into a tizzy.

As soon as Emily walked into her office, Anthony followed behind her and closed the door. "So?" he asked.

"So, what?"

"Come on, Em. Don't make me beg you for the details. How was last night?"

"The turtle hatch was a success," Emily replied with an impish grin on her face.

"Really? That's great news, but you know that's not what I meant."

"Okay, I'll spill. It was great. Mike was fascinated by the turtles, and after finishing with the volunteers, he came back to my place for a drink."

"And?"

"And he asked me out for dinner tomorrow night. There might've been an innocent kiss good night."

"Yes!" Anthony replied with a fist pump. "Jane and I were so hopeful when Mike volunteered to drive you home. He seems like a great guy. He gets two thumbs up from Marc and me."

Emily sat there smiling in agreement.

"Also, Marc says you owe him another trivia night. We ended up coming in second by only a few points."

"Tell him it's a deal. That place was awesome. The food was delicious too," Emily said.

Abigail, the receptionist, called over the intercom to announce the first appointment of the morning—Jasmine, an itchy Shih Tzu with chronic allergies. Emily's patients kept her occupied all day, so it was almost closing time before she checked her messages. Having just missed a call from Duncan, she dialed him back right away.

"Hi, Em."

"Hey, Duncan. Did you get my message?"

"I did, but I'm swamped with work. Sorry."

"I understand, but what's going on at Mrs. Klein's house?" Emily asked.

Duncan hesitated before answering.

"Sarah Klein asked me to monitor the house for her. Should I call her to find out what's happening?" Emily asked pointedly.

"Okay, you win, but you need to keep it to yourself for now."

"I promise."

"The private pathologist that Sarah Klein hired, along with the medical examiner, has determined the cause of death. Mrs. Klein died of nicotine poisoning."

"What? We all know smoking is a deadly habit, but is it possible to poison yourself from the nicotine in cigarettes?" Emily asked.

"No, that's just it. It's impossible to reach these high levels by smoking alone. The crime scene techs are bagging up all the food, medicine, vitamins and personal care items in her house to see if we can find the source."

"I've heard that if you use those nicotine patches to quit smoking, but then keep on smoking anyway, it can be dangerous," Emily said.

"It can, but those symptoms are usually mild and rarely cause sudden illness. Her daughter confirmed she had no interest in quitting smoking, so had no need for nicotine patches. Based on what you told me, she seemed perfectly fine until she died."

"Were her nicotine levels really that high?"

"Off the charts. The M.E. thinks she must have ingested it right before her death based on the analysis of her stomach contents. Assuming this is a case of poisoning, we're proceeding to treat her death as an official homicide investigation."

Those words hung in the air like a heavy cloud. Emily was still trying to process this news when she pondered out loud. "Who would want to kill Mrs. Klein? It makes no sense. She was a piano teacher who volunteered with animal charities."

"Things aren't always as they seem. There's a motive, and we're going to figure it out. Listen, Em, I've got to go. You, okay?"

"No, I'm not okay. Does Sarah know about this yet?"

"I hung up with her right before calling you. She's pretty upset," Duncan said.

"I'll try to call her later today. Are you okay if I tell Anthony? I don't think I'll be able to keep it from him, anyway. You know he won't tell anyone."

"Okay, but only the two of you. If this gets out, there'll be hell to pay."

"Pinky swear," she replied while brandishing her smallest digit in the phone's direction as a sign of solidarity.

Emily was pretty shaken up by the news, making it impossible to hide her true feelings from Anthony. Once she filled him in on the details of her conversation with Duncan, they both decided they would get together after work. Rehashing all the events that had occurred since their house call to Mrs. Klein was their best chance to uncover any previously overlooked details. Marc had to work late, so Anthony volunteered to bring over dinner after the hospital closed. Emily contemplated making a meal from her fridge full of healthy ingredients but didn't have the energy to even offer. Takeout was perfect.

"Okay, you get to pick; Italian, Chinese, BBQ or Peruvian?" Anthony asked. "I'm leaving now. I'll run home to change and will pick up dinner on my way."

"Ooh, BBQ sounds great. Are you thinking about Sunny's Pit BBQ? I love that place, especially their fried pickles and okra."

"Sounds good to me. Don't forget about their cornbread muffins. Marc's specialty is grilled chicken on a quinoa salad. I can't complain when someone will make me a delicious, healthy meal, but I need some comfort food tonight," Anthony said.

"Ditto. I'll be leaving soon too. If I'm walking Elvis on the beach when you get there, use your key to let yourself in."

· · ·

Tears often flow at the most inopportune moment—as if they have a mind of their own. Emily tried to hold hers back during the drive home, but to no avail. By the time she pulled in to her driveway, she was sobbing. It was difficult to face the reality that Mrs. Klein had been murdered. Elvis, who was sitting in the front seat beside her, was a stark reminder of her role in the case. She was smack dab in the middle of things. After walking into her cottage, Emily took a few deep breaths, and then splashed her face with cold water, attempting to reset her emotions. She tended to Elvis and Bella's culinary needs and still had enough time to mix up a batch of her famous margaritas before Anthony arrived.

"That smells so good. I'm starving. Do you want to eat outside?" Emily called out as Anthony let himself in the front door.

"For sure. Looks like we're going to have a gorgeous sunset," Anthony said before turning the corner to join Emily in the kitchen. He took one look at her face, set the food on the counter, and reached out to give her a hug. Clearly, she had been crying.

"I'm sorry, Em."

"Me too," she replied while accepting his supporting embrace. "I need a few minutes before we talk about Mrs. Klein. Let's eat first." Anthony nodded in agreement.

Emily poured him a margarita, and after filling their plates and then their stomachs, they sat back to enjoy the last moments of the day. The sun was an enormous ball of fire painting plumes of orange and red across the sky. They sipped their cocktails while staring at the sunset, hoping to see the elusive green flash. Legend says that during the exact moment when the sun drops below the horizon over the ocean, a green flash of light can streak across the sky. They'd been staring at sunsets all their lives. Anthony swears he saw the green flash once in high school, but Emily was always skeptical. However, it didn't keep her from hoping her turn was next.

Emily's phone rang, ruining her sunset Zen moment. She contemplated not answering the call, but then changed her mind. "Hello."

"Hi, Emily. It's Mike Lane."

Emily immediately sat up straight and ran her fingers through her hair to comb out the knots, as if he could see her.

"Hi, Mike."

"Sorry, it's so late, but I wondered if you were still open for dinner tomorrow night? I totally understand if you've made plans already."

"Tomorrow is great. Did you have a place in mind?"

"I was hoping you could recommend one. I'm still getting my bearings."

"There's a great beach restaurant near my place. It's super casual, and they have live music on Saturdays."

"Sounds perfect to me. How about I pick you up at seven o'clock?" Mike said.

"Great. See you tomorrow." Emily hung up from her call and turned to face Anthony, who was squirming in his chair, physically prompting her for more details.

"So, where are you taking him tomorrow?"

"Why? Are you going to show up to spy on us?" Emily laughed.

"No, you've got this."

"I was thinking of Barnacles Seafood Shack. It's casual enough, so there's less pressure on the date."

"This is big, Em. I'm happy for you."

"Thanks," Emily replied before turning to watch the last moments of the sunset, to recapture that Zen feeling.

"I thought you were going to ask him about the nicotine poisoning." Anthony said.

"I told Duncan that I wouldn't tell anyone, besides you, of course. The last thing I want is for him to get in trouble."

"My brain hurts trying to think of anyone who would want to kill Mrs. Klein," Anthony said. "This means we could have a murderer on the loose in Coral Shores. It's kind of freaking me out."

Emily was so wrapped up in her own emotions she had overlooked the potential risk to the community. Until Duncan and Mike arrested the person responsible, she would not feel safe. Deciding to wait until tomorrow to press Duncan for more details seemed like a wise decision. Her next call was to check in with Sarah, who had seemed open to talk about her mom and the investigation. Duncan would eventually forgive her if she overstepped her bounds. Plus, Anthony would not leave for the night until he had the latest update.

"Sarah, it's Emily Benton. I hope this is a good time?"

"Sure. Is everything okay?"

"Yes, Elvis is wonderful. No change there. I was calling to check on you. I understand you got some bad news today."

There was a pause and Emily thought she could hear Sarah sniffle before she replied. "I'm really not doing very well. Thinking about the fact that someone murdered my mom makes me feel sick. I can't even grasp saying that word, *murder*. Every time I close my eyes, I see something horrible happening to her."

There were no words Emily could offer to ease her pain. Sarah was having difficulty talking through her grief, so Emily waited a minute before adding, "Is there anything I can do for you?"

"I don't think so, but thank you for offering. Now that they know what killed her, things will move faster as they search for the likely source of the poison. My pathologist said they may have results within a day or two."

"I guess that's the next step in trying to solve this," Emily agreed. "I haven't been around your mom for the past few years, but I can't imagine any reason someone would want to hurt her."

"Whoever did this will face justice. Now that I know what happened, I'm using all my resources to find out who's responsible. When I get my mind set on something, I can ruffle a few feathers. I don't care this time."

"I totally understand and would feel the same way. Detective Lane and my brother will keep working day and night until they solve this."

"I know they will, but I can't sit back and do nothing. My goal is to help with the investigation, not to get in everyone's way. Tomorrow morning, there's a planned conference call with the forensic team that's working on my mom's computer cloud account. Fingers crossed they've uncovered something helpful."

Emily didn't know what else to say. She was feeling helpless, but not hopeless. Sarah Klein was a force to be reckoned with, and her mighty resources were bound to turn up a clue.

"Emily, I've got to get ready for dinner now, but I'll be in touch. Thanks for checking in on me. You're very kind."

"If you ever need to talk, call me anytime," Emily said before hanging up.

"That sounded intense." Anthony's brow was furrowed and his lips were pursed together. He was clearly worried.

"It was. I think she's struggling to accept that anyone would have wanted to hurt her mom."

"Well, of course she is. I can't accept it, so I can't even imagine how she's feeling," Anthony said.

"I also think she's gone from being sad to being angry. She wants the guilty party to be held responsible for what they did, and she's going to push hard for results."

"And she should. Fingers crossed that Duncan and Mike can solve this case before anyone else gets hurt."

While considering the potential risk to the community, they both sat in silence for a few minutes. Coral Shores was a small town that prided itself on its safe and friendly atmosphere. Serious crimes were almost unheard of. Emily was glad that Mike had moved here from a big city, bringing with him the experience needed to solve dangerous crimes.

Elvis brought Emily and Anthony out of their private thoughts when he jumped up on the chaise lounge, demanding some attention.

"Hey, buddy," Anthony said while reaching over to pet him. "I just realized I haven't heard him cough in days."

"Yeah, I've been reducing his medicine and so far, no relapse."

"Does that mean you're going to put him up for adoption?"

"Not yet. I'll wait until he's been off his meds for a while before I make that decision. Plus, it makes me too sad to think about it."

"I noticed Bella avoids us when Elvis is around. She's been watching us from her window perch, but any other night, she would have been out here," Anthony said.

"I know. That's why I can't put off this decision about Elvis forever. It's not fair to Bella."

"I'm sorry, Em. I'd take him for a few days, but you know my apartment doesn't allow pets. Such a stupid rule, but they're pretty strict about enforcing it."

"It's okay. I think being at the beach is making Elvis feel more at home."

"You know, Marc and I have been talking about maybe moving in together. Marc's townhouse is awesome and they allow pets. You never know?"

"Really? I'm so happy for both of you," Emily exclaimed while jumping up to give Anthony a hug. "That's a huge step, but it totally makes sense to me. Are you nervous?"

"No, not really. I'm excited. If you'd asked me six months ago what I would be doing with my life, I never could have imagined being back in Coral Shores, in a great relationship, and working with my best friend. Life is strange that way."

"Well, I'm glad you're here, and I think Marc is awesome."

"Thanks, Em. We've only started talking about our plans, so don't mention anything about it to Jane or the staff, okay?"

"Got it."

"We've got a busy Saturday morning scheduled, and you need your beauty sleep before your big date," Anthony said. "I'm going home, but I'm taking my leftovers with me. Perfect for lunch tomorrow."

"Thanks for getting dinner, Anthony. Do you mind if I stay out here?"

"You don't need to show me out, Em. We're a little beyond those formalities. Night."

Emily sat for a while on her lounge chair, petting Elvis until she could hear his soft snores. It took some time, but she was feeling more at home in her mom's cottage. It was slowly becoming Emily's place. Her mom's presence became the warm backdrop that Emily used to create her own fresh memories, but it no longer dominated every moment or space. She was grateful that her mom had left her a home filled with so much love to carry her forward in life.

CHAPTER NINE

Saturday arrived like a hurricane. It was nonstop from the moment Emily stepped foot in the hospital. Being a successful veterinarian required an innate ability to multitask. Celebrating with families bringing new puppies and kittens in for their first checkup was in sharp contrast to when she had to deliver a difficult diagnosis to a pet owner who was struggling to see their beloved dog or cat in diminishing health. All the while, she still had staff to manage and patients to monitor. Emily's commitment to her clients and their furry family members was unwavering, but the emotional drain was something she struggled to manage. Anthony lightened that load. The clients, pets and staff loved him, and his leadership had become an important part of Emily's success at the hospital. They made a great team.

Closing time was earlier on Saturdays, and Emily was wrapping up her day when Anthony joined her in the office.

"Mrs. Martinez has left with Kensington. The emergency hospital has all of his records. She was hoping to transfer Kensington back here when we reopen on Monday if he still needs to be in the hospital."

"Sounds good. I'll check with the emergency hospital tomorrow for an update." Kensington was a twelve-year-old Bichon Frise who was being treated for kidney failure. He'd started eating again, which was an encouraging sign, but since the Coral Shores Veterinary Hospital was now closed until Monday, he needed to have his vital signs monitored while staying on his IV fluids. The nearby emergency hospital could care for him during that time.

"Have you heard from Duncan about the case?"

"No, and I've been too busy to call him."

"I'm wrapping up some inventory paperwork, so I'll be here another hour or two. Are you close to finishing?"

"Almost. When I get home, I'm going to take Elvis for a long walk, and then I have a few things to prep for tomorrow. Mac and Ava are coming over in the morning. I can't wait."

"Big weekend, Em. Date tonight with your handsome detective—"

"He's not *my* detective," she said, interrupting him.

Anthony ignored her and continued. "And a play date with your niece and nephew. I'm proud of you."

Emily knew he was happy she wasn't whiling away her time all alone like she'd been doing ever since her mom died. It felt good to have plans for the weekend.

"Let's go, Elvis," she said, and then followed his bouncing step out the back door.

．．．

It was a hot one today. Emily and Elvis cooled down in the ocean after their walk. Elvis would run in and out of the surf to chase the waves while Emily waded nearby so she could keep an eye on him. A lazy afternoon on the beach was exactly what she needed. The ocean really could heal all wounds.

Motivated by her recent grocery purchase, Emily prepared a delicious grilled chicken salad and a mango and berry smoothie for lunch. She still needed to get some kid-friendly food for tomorrow's playdate, so after confirming Bengle's offered Sunday delivery, she sat down at the computer and filled her virtual shopping cart: watermelon, carrot sticks and veggie dip, juice boxes, hotdogs, freezer fruit pops, cheesy crackers and ice cream. It was an aunt's prerogative to spoil the kids.

Even though Emily planned to wear a sundress for her date, she put on another pair of her mom's favorite flip-flops. They were royal blue, with tiny daisies adorning the straps. Going to a beachfront restaurant in south Florida meant there was no need to dress up. She took the time to blow dry her hair and even put on a little makeup. While staring back at her reflection in the mirror, it was impossible for her to deny she was the spitting image of her mom, and that made her smile.

Emily needed a pep talk before her big date, and she knew exactly whom to call. "Do you have time to chat?" Emily asked after Jane answered the phone.

"Sure. I was about to call you. The kids are in swim lessons right now. What's up?"

"Mike will be here soon for our date. I'm feeling a little nervous."

"That's good."

"Why would that be good?" Emily asked.

"It means that you like him. When was the last time you said that about a first date?"

"Too long, for sure." Emily had a few serious boyfriends over the years, but that seemed like a lifetime ago. Her mom was her only priority over the past year, and after she died, Emily jumped right into hospital ownership. There was no time for anything else, especially dating.

"Just be yourself, Em, and have fun."

"Thanks, Jane. I needed to hear that. Are you still planning to drop Mac and Ava off tomorrow around eleven o'clock?"

"That's the plan. They're so excited. It's going to be impossible to get them to sleep tonight. They keep talking about building a sandcastle dog house for Elvis. Thanks again for doing this. Duncan and I have planned a round of golf with friends and an early dinner date. We should be back at your place by eight o'clock to pick them up."

"Sounds good. I'm glad you're getting some adult-only time. I can't promise you I won't return the kids in a sugar haze."

"No worries. They'll be so tired after swimming all day and running around on the beach that nothing will keep them from crashing asleep."

"I'll see you tomorrow. I think I'm going to sit on the deck with a small glass of wine until Mike gets here. Settle the nerves and all."

"Have fun. I expect details in the morning," Jane said before hanging up.

Emily was expecting Mike to knock at the door any minute now when her phone rang—it was Sarah Klein.

"Hi, Sarah. Is everything okay?"

"I'm not sure. I was wondering if you could help me with something?"

"Sure, if I can," Emily replied.

"Was your mom or have you been approached by any realtors trying to buy your cottage?" Sarah asked.

"No, and my mom would have mentioned something like that."

"Hmmm." Sarah paused before continuing. "My forensic team has found something on mom's computer that's leaving me feeling unsettled."

"What's that?" Emily asked.

"A real estate company had been sending mom direct communications trying to buy her property. It looks like they may have come to the house on one or two occasions. She turned them down flat, but subsequent emails became more forceful."

"How so?"

"Well, they kept upping their offer, and it appears after the last time Mom refused to sell, they threatened her—not physically, but with aggressive tactics. They said they owned the land next to her cottage and planned to build a large home right up to the property line. It looks like they were going to mount a legal challenge to her current property setbacks and beach access. It was all extremely veiled, but the overall message was clear. Sell to them or she would regret it."

"What's the name of the company?"

"The Good Life Real Estate Company. Have you heard of them?"

"Their signs are everywhere; on billboards, local TV ads and park benches. I think they're behind many of the old historic beach cottage tear-downs where giant, ugly mansions now stand."

"I'm doing a little research on the company right now. It's despicable that they would try to intimidate a senior citizen into selling their home. Obviously, they hadn't met my mother. She was tough as nails and nothing ever scared her."

Emily smiled while thinking about Mrs. Klein telling off some sleazy real estate developer. While she finished that thought, there was a knock at the door. Mike was here.

"Sarah, can I call you back tomorrow? Someone's at the door."

"Sure, Emily. I'll be around all day. Thanks."

"Okay, Emily. Be cool," she said under her breath before opening the door. That was easier said than done once she saw Mike standing there. He looked so good in his upscale surfer polo shirt, shorts, flip-flops and retro Ray-Bans.

"Hi, Emily. You look really nice."

"Thanks, you too. I mean, it's nice to see you without a holster on your belt."

Mike laughed. "It feels weird sometimes not to have it on, but I'm looking forward to tonight."

"Me too. Come on in. I'll grab my purse and then we can go."

It amazed Emily when Elvis calmly sauntered over to greet Mike, not at all feeling the need to posture and bark. "I think Elvis really likes you," she said. "He usually embarrasses himself by charging at the door like an attack dog."

"I grew up with dogs, and cats too. My mom was involved with a local rescue group, and we were always fostering some wayward animal. Of course, many of them became family members."

"I think I'd like your mom," Emily said.

"And I'm sure she'd like you," Mike said, smiling.

"Okay, you two. Be good." Emily was, of course, speaking to Bella and Elvis. Bella attempted to lift her head, acknowledging their departure, and Elvis retreated to the large pillow at the end of the couch.

. . .

Barnacles was busy for a Saturday night. The waterfront seafood restaurant was having one of their infamous full moon parties. The band was set up outside on the deck, and some local buskers were performing in front of the restaurant on the public beach. A drum circle had formed and stilt walkers, people in costume, and balloon artists moved amongst the crowd. They were fortunate to get a table overlooking the festivities.

"I totally forgot about the fact it was a full moon today. It's a little over the top," Emily said, concerned that she'd made a mistake picking Barnacles for their first date.

"This is awesome. Do they have a party every full moon?" Mike asked.

"Yup, unless a hurricane comes ashore on the same day."

After being seated, the waitress came by, touting the chef's specials. Emily chose the blackened Mahi tacos, and Mike jumped at the chance to sample all the local delicacies when he ordered the seafood lover's platter. They were sipping their rumrunner cocktails while waiting for their food when Mike brought up the subject of the investigation.

"Emily, I want to let you know Duncan told me he updated you and Anthony on the cause of death for Eliza Klein. I'm okay with it.

As long as both of you understand, we must keep it private for the time being."

Emily nodded in the affirmative. "We'd never jeopardize your case or betray a confidence. I hope you know that."

"I do."

"Duncan also told me it's now an official homicide investigation," Emily said.

"It is."

Once again, Mike was unwilling to divulge any details, so Emily thought twice before asking another question. In the end, she couldn't help herself. "Do you have any leads on the source of the poison? Any suspects yet?"

"We're working on a few theories, but still waiting to get the forensics back from all the food items we collected at her house."

"I've been in contact with Sarah Klein and wanted you to know—full disclosure and all. Most of the time we talk about Elvis, but she's also confided in me about her mom's case."

"That's understandable. She's a formidable lady. I wasn't certain at first, but now I'm impressed by the private forensic company she's hired. They've been working in tandem with the M.E. which is only helping to move the case along at a faster pace."

"She's anxious to start planning a funeral for her mom. I can't imagine dealing with her grief and then having to navigate all these hurdles with the police on top of everything else," Emily said.

"Hopefully, we can release her mom's body soon. Emily, I can't talk about the case right now. I hope you can understand and respect that?"

She didn't have to like it, but she could respect it. Plus, this was a first date, and Emily wanted to relax and enjoy her handsome, charming companion.

"Okay, I promise. No more questions."

As their food arrived, the band started playing. The salty sea air was the backdrop for the tropical island-style country music; a little Zac Brown and Kenny Chesney sprinkled in with some classic

Jimmy Buffett. Emily couldn't imagine why she'd been so nervous before this date. Mike was easy to talk to. He was funny and a good listener. They shared a slice of key lime pie for dessert before joining the full moon party on the beach. The performers had garnered a large crowd of spectators as Emily and Mike floated from one group to the next. Mike suggested they go for a walk since he needed help to digest his huge dinner. Emily involuntarily held her breath when Mike took her hand in his as they approached the historic pier and turnaround point.

"Living in a short-term corporate apartment is wearing thin but until now, I didn't know where to look." Mike continued to hold her hand but stepped in front, turning to face her. "I've started searching for places to rent or buy near the beach, and I have you to thank for that."

"Really?" Emily tried to reign in her excitement, attempting to play it cool, but no luck. "I'm glad I could show you the way. I don't understand anyone who doesn't want to live at the beach."

"What about Duncan?" Mike asked as they resumed their walk.

"Okay, I understand why his place is great for a young family. Jane and Duncan have a beautiful home. It's just not for me."

"I'd like having a golf course in my backyard, but I prefer the water. Would you be interested in seeing a few places with me? I can figure out the real estate part, but it would be great to have an insider's opinion on the location."

"Sure. Anytime." It was a good thing the sun was setting because it helped camouflage Emily's blushing cheeks. It was always impossible for her to hide her emotions, and she was over-the-top excited about the prospect of having Mike living nearby. After making their way back to the restaurant, Emily invited him to join her for a nightcap at her place. He happily accepted.

. . .

Back at Emily's, they both greeted Elvis and Bella with pets and treats before moving outside to the beach deck. Emily poured herself a glass of wine, but Mike opted for water since he had to drive home. He'd once again taken over her mom's chaise lounge, but this time, he invited Emily to join him. She was sitting in front of Mike, resting her back against his chest, with his very muscular arms wrapped around her body. He smelled so good.

"Duncan told me your niece and nephew are coming over tomorrow. That should be a blast."

"Yeah, it's been too long since they've had a beach day with their favorite aunt." An extended period of silence followed Emily's reply. Their mutual attraction was obvious, but Mike seemed somewhat guarded or reluctant to act on those feelings. It made sense since she was his coworker's sister, and he must have felt the weight of that. Plus, Emily was clueless about his recent relationship status. Maybe he was on the rebound? That possibility didn't stop her from sitting on the edge of the chair so she could turn to face him. Saying nothing, they both leaned in for a kiss that slowly morphed into a passionate embrace. Mike pulled Emily into his arms, slowly kissing her neck. They were approaching a point of no return when Mike sat back, smiling at Emily.

She returned his gaze but added an impish, "What?"

"You are a surprise, Emily Benton."

"A good surprise, I hope."

"Very good. I know you have a big day tomorrow with the kids, and I think if I stay any longer, I won't be able to leave."

"That wouldn't be the worst thing." Emily was smiling and despite her desire to continue their date, it was wise to hit the pause button. He was her brother's partner and that complicated things.

"Can we make plans to get together this week? You can let me know what day is good for you, and I'll make it work."

Emily sat up, struggling to pull herself away from Mike's embrace. "I'd love that. I'll look at my schedule on Monday and can pick a day that looks light."

All the endorphins racing through her body caused Emily's legs to wobble as they walked hand in hand to her front door. After a long, heated kiss good night, Emily was out of breath as she watched Mike drive away in his car.

Bella and Elvis gave her a strange look when she walked back into the cottage and exclaimed, "Best first date ever!" She brought both of her furry roommates onto the deck so she could finish her wine and bask in the remnants of Mike's presence. She couldn't wait for date number two.

CHAPTER TEN

Waking up without the help of an alarm clock was one of life's simple pleasures. Emily loved easing into her day, avoiding the mad dash to get out the door on time. The weather was going to be sunny with a light breeze and a gentle surf—perfect for Mac and Ava to swim in the ocean. After taking care of Elvis and Bella's breakfast, she was savoring her morning coffee on the deck. The faint scent of Mike's shampoo or soap still lingered in the air as she lounged on her mom's chair. It smelled even better than the fragrant gardenias that bordered the garden.

"Okay, Emily. You've got stuff to do," she said to herself after scarfing down a quick bowl of cereal. The goal was to set up all the beach toys before the kids arrived. Her mom had a shed full of boogie boards, pails and shovels, frisbees, beach balls, sand chairs and a large shade awning for a day in the sun. An automated text announced the imminent arrival of the Bengle's delivery, so after the cooler was prepped, Emily made a mental note to lock Elvis in the bedroom before answering the door.

Emily was eager to speak with Sarah, and frustrated with the time change. It was still too early to call her in California. She had been thinking about the Good Life Real Estate Company ever since their conversation last night. It was easy to hate what this big developer was doing to their town, and the revelation they were pressuring Mrs. Klein into a sale was unconscionable.

The monstrosities they built on the beach detracted from the charming personality of Coral Shores. In Emily's opinion, more wasn't always better. She remembered her mom complaining about the rising property taxes as these huge, expensive mansions drove up the real estate market, while adding nothing redeeming to the community. The homes often sat empty most of the year since they were owned by wealthy out-of-towners who did not contribute to the local culture and economy.

After making a quick call over to the emergency veterinary hospital, Emily was happy to learn that Kensington was going to be discharged. His appetite and kidney values had continued to improve, which was great news. Hearing that he had become a little ornery with the vet techs meant he was acting more like his usual self. She would call Kensington's owner on Monday to schedule a follow-up.

The Bengle's grocery delivery van pulled up to her curb right on time. She sprinted to grab Elvis and secure him in her bedroom before he went on alert. A quick glance out the window confirmed it was Bucky approaching her front door.

He knocked and before Emily could answer, he shouted, "Is that attack dog of yours locked up?"

Emily was not amused when she opened the door. "I told Mr. Bengle he wouldn't be out when you delivered, and he's not. Please set the groceries on the floor."

"Your choice." Bucky peered into her living room as he put the bags down. "You must have told Mr. Bengle a good story to keep him from kicking you off the delivery list," he said, with contempt.

"He was very understanding. He also told me you didn't have any injuries from that day. I'm glad. I was very sorry that it happened, even if Elvis didn't cause a bite wound."

The moment Emily said Elvis's name, Bucky's demeanor changed. The smug look washed from his face, and he seemed to shrink in stature.

"Your dog's name is Elvis?" Bucky asked.

Emily nodded yes, but chose not to elaborate. He had a confused look on his face and before she could reply; he turned around and was making a hasty retreat to his delivery van.

"Thanks," Emily shouted from the doorway, then said to herself, "That was strange." Figuring out the mental gymnastics of a guy like Bucky was not a worthwhile use of her time, so she grabbed the groceries and closed the door.

Emily could hear Elvis grunting, and as soon as she released him from lock-up, he raced to the front door with laser focus; hackles up, growling and sniffing around the threshold. She'd only ever seen him act this way in the presence of Bucky. Elvis knew the delivery man had been here, and he wasn't happy about it.

"What is it with you and that guy?" Emily asked Elvis. Nothing she did could distract him from his patrol of the front entry, so she turned her attention to the groceries to get everything in the cooler for the beach picnic.

Elvis had diffused his anxious energy and had been calm for a while when Duncan, Jane and the kids pulled into the driveway. Emily was contemplating whether she should secure him until everyone was inside the house, but his ears were forward, tail was wagging, and he was happily jumping up and down. She had no concerns he would be anything other than his friendly, sweet self, but held him in her arms, just in case.

"Elvis!" Mac and Ava shouted and ran over to greet the happy terrier, who started spinning and dancing with joy the moment Emily set him on the floor. She was quite aware of the fact that today's beach visit was all about the dog and less about their favorite aunt.

"The kids brought a gift for Elvis. Hope you don't mind," Jane said. "They wanted him to have his own doggie-sized soccer ball."

"That's sweet."

Jane pulled Emily into the kitchen for a private conversation. "So, how was it?"

"Incredible. I'm worried if I say too much, I'll jinx it. We're going out again this week."

"Oh, Em. I'm so happy for you." Jane gave her a celebratory squeeze. "Is he a good kisser?"

"Jane," Emily said, feigning indignation before smiling and adding, "Amazing."

"I knew it. I could just tell. He's sexy, Em. Not as sexy as Duncan, though."

"Ew," Emily replied.

"Okay, you can give me the rest of the details later. We're cutting it close for our tee time." Jane said. "Kids, come over here for a second. Let's go over the rules for today."

As Jane was laying down the law, Emily pulled Duncan onto the beach deck.

"I want to let you know I cleared the air with Mike last night and promised to keep all the facts of the case confidential." Emily said.

"I know you will," Duncan replied, while turning his head to face the water, avoiding eye contact with Emily.

"What are you hiding, Duncan? I can tell by the look on your face. You know you can't keep stuff from me."

There was an extended silence while he continued to stare off at the ocean. "Em, you need to stay out of this investigation."

"I'm right in the middle of this investigation, in case you forgot. Sarah Klein called me last night and updated me on the fact that her mom was being harassed by a real estate developer. Did you know that?"

"Of course, I did. It's my job to know." Emily could tell he was getting annoyed.

"Well, I have to call her back tonight. She'll know about whatever the forensic specialist has turned up and she'll probably tell me. I'd prefer to hear it from you."

Duncan's shoulders dropped and in a defeated tone he said, "The poison was in her orange juice."

That last sentence hung in the air. Emily was trying to make sense of it and began pacing around the deck before asking, "Do you know if it was from groceries she'd ordered from Bengle's?"

"That's what we're in the process of determining. We only found out about the source of the poison this morning."

"You don't think Mr. Bengle has anything to do with this, do you? He seems like the nicest man."

"Right now, we still need to confirm where she bought the container of juice. One step at a time."

"I'm pretty sure it was from Bengle's. She didn't drive, and she had a fridge full of prepared organic groceries. Bengle's is the only place I can think of that delivers that type of stuff."

"We still need to complete our due diligence," Duncan said. "I've got to go now. Thanks again for taking the kids today. It's all they've been talking about all week. I'll text you when we're on our way to pick them up later."

Emily wanted to keep pushing Duncan for more information, but she needed to put this disturbing revelation out of her mind, at least for the rest of the day. Mac and Ava deserved her full attention. Emily was good at compartmentalizing things when necessary, so she would wait until tonight to speak with Sarah. Maybe Duncan would have more to share when he returned.

As soon as Duncan and Jane left, Emily turned to the kids and said, "Okay, you two. Are you ready for our beach party?"

Bella was startled off her perch when Mac shouted his reply. "Yes, Auntie Em!"

"Can Elvis come to the party, too?" Ava asked.

"Absolutely. Playing on the beach is Elvis's favorite thing to do."

"Me too," Mac added.

"Mommy already put on our sunscreen. Can we go now?" Ava was jumping up and down in anticipation.

"To the beach!" Emily declared.

The day was a blast. Between playing in the gentle waves and then chasing Elvis up and down the shore, it was constant laughs and giggles. The kids spent an hour building a sand dog castle. Elvis contributed by digging holes around the castle, which were then incorporated into a moat for his Highness, King Elvis. The seashells Ava collected were used to adorn the palace. Mac wrote Elvis's name in the sand in case any passersby on the beach wondered who lived there.

Other than a short time-out in the shade to eat their lunch, it was go-go-go. By late afternoon, Emily could tell everyone had enough sun and play for the day. Ava had become quiet and every time she slowly blinked her eyes, Emily wondered if they were going to open again. The kids were a big help to bring all the beach equipment back to the house. Emily was thankful her mom had installed an outdoor shower a few years ago. It was easy to get rid of the sand and salt that encrusted them from head to toe.

"I'm hungry, Auntie Em," Mac said.

"I have hotdogs for dinner. Sound good?" she asked.

Ava wasn't very subtle when she asked, "What about after the hotdogs?"

"Well, there might be some ice cream sandwiches in the freezer."

"Yay!"

After dinner, they moved to the living room to watch cartoons. Ava immediately fell asleep on the couch, Elvis curled up at her feet. Mac sat on the floor petting Bella, who was perched on a pillow beside him. Emily thought they were the cutest things ever. Emily texted Jane to let her know to come in without knocking when they arrived, so they didn't wake Ava and send Elvis into a greeting frenzy.

Her mom's presence weighed on Emily as she sat in another of her mom's favorite chairs, watching the kids. She had never planned to return to Coral Shores after vet school, but that was proof of the hubris of youth, assuming you know everything before life's journey had even begun. Emily was certain her world was bigger than Coral Shores until it wasn't. She pictured herself working at a big city specialty hospital and living in an industrial urban loft apartment. It was the opposite of where she ended up.

Today would have been one of her mom's favorite days— spending time at the beach with her grandkids. Seeing the wonder in their eyes as they built their sandcastle or caught their first wave on the boogie boards. It made Emily sad to think that maybe the kids were too young to hold on to any memories of their grandmother. Emily made a promise to herself to never forget how she felt right now. Building a life in Coral Shores made perfect sense, considering the day she'd had. This small oceanfront hamlet was plenty big enough, after all. Losing her mom made her realize how important family was and that meant staying close to Duncan, Jane and the kids. Anthony and Marc were fast becoming her honorary family, and even though they weren't blood relatives, the bond was equally strong.

Elvis's ears perked up when he heard Duncan's car pull into the driveway, but even he was too tired from his day at the beach to do anything about it. Jane tiptoed through the front door, joining Emily in the living room.

"Just as expected," Jane said while smiling down at her kids. "Thanks, Em,"

"No, thank you for sharing them with me."

A minute later, Duncan came into the cottage, hanging up from a phone call as he entered the room.

"Good job, sis," Duncan said with a whisper. "It's not easy to wear them out. Looks like Elvis had a big day, too."

Emily smiled, then asked, "How was golf?"

"Well, my score was horrible, but I didn't care. We needed today, Em. Thanks," Jane replied.

Duncan bent down to pick up Ava. She didn't even raise an eyelid, sleeping through the entire transition from the front door to the car. Emily realized that now was not the time to ask Duncan questions about Mrs. Klein, but resolved to call him tomorrow for more info.

"Come on, Mac. Time to go," Jane whispered to her son as she gathered up their beach bags.

"Thanks, Auntie Em. I had the most fun. Promise we can come and see Elvis this week. Bella, too."

"I'll talk to your mom and we'll see what we can figure out." Mac gave her one of those looks that said *you're telling me something you think I want to hear because I'm a kid, but you aren't going to do what you said*. Emily replied to his fleeting look with a resounding, "I promise."

"Okay, remember, you promised," Mac said.

Emily executed a combination of a pinky swear and a Girl Scout salute with her hands, clearly communicating she was good on her word. That seemed to be enough to convince Mac she was telling the truth.

Once the kids had gone, Emily grabbed a big glass of ice water and carried her massive cat out to the chaise lounge. Elvis was still snoring on the couch, so it was a good time to give Bella some undivided attention. She was still trying to process the news that Duncan had shared with her this morning. *The poison was in the orange juice.* Emily didn't order any orange juice from Bengle's, but she was certain she would have tossed it in the garbage if she had. Hopefully, Sarah Klein had more information to share with her. It was time to make a call.

"Hi, Sarah. It's Emily. Sorry I had to cut our conversation short last night."

"No problem at all. How's Elvis?"

"He's asleep on the couch. My niece and nephew were over today and we played on the beach all day. They wore each other out, but he had so much fun."

"I can picture him running around in his element. Do your niece and nephew have a dog of their own?"

It was obvious where Sarah was going with this question, shocking Emily that she hadn't thought of it herself. "No, they don't, but they sure love Elvis."

"Is there any chance they would be interested in adopting him?"

"I don't know. My sister-in-law had a dog when she married my brother, but he passed away right before the kids were born. I think with Duncan's busy schedule and two young kids, it wasn't something that had come up again."

"Well, I thought I would ask. I'm still consumed with guilt about having to leave Elvis behind. Hearing how well he's doing in your home helps me sleep at night. Thank you again for taking care of him."

"You're welcome. It's been fun having him here," Emily said before pausing. She was contemplating how to address the real reason for her call. "In the strictest of confidence, Duncan told me they found the source of the nicotine poisoning. I'm so sorry, Sarah."

"At first, I was debilitated by my grief, but now I'm mad as hell. Someone's going to pay for what they did to my mom."

"Have there been any new leads or suspects?" Emily asked.

"That part of the investigation is in the hands of the police now, which I guess is Detective Lane and your brother. My forensic team can't investigate the crime or question witnesses, so I have to be patient."

"I know it's hard being so far away, but they won't rest until they sort this out. I believe that with all my heart."

"Do you know this local grocery store, Bengle's?" Sarah asked. "We believe that's where she was getting all her groceries."

"Not really. I found out about them indirectly through your mom." Emily hesitated while she contemplated telling Sarah about her meeting with Mr. Bengle and Elvis's repeated encounters with Bucky. She decided it was time for full disclosure.

After Emily had finished her story, Sarah said, "This means something. Elvis is a smart dog. Why else would he keep acting that way unless this delivery guy was not a good person?"

"Bucky is a rough character. Maybe he had an encounter with Elvis when he delivered to your mom's place? I'm pretty sure he doesn't like dogs."

"I wish I could call her up and ask her. My mom has always been my sounding board. She had the most practical advice and could always set me straight. My heart feels like it's going to break in half some days."

"My mom was that person for me, too. It's really hard when the only person you feel you can turn to is no longer there," Emily said. "Is there anything I can do to help?"

"Thanks, Emily. You've already been an enormous help, and I always feel better after we talk. While the investigation about the source of the poison is in the hands of the police right now, my forensic team is still sorting through my mom's files about this real estate developer. I've also been working with our family friend, Mr. VanKleef, who was also mom's lawyer. Last month, she changed her will, adding new provisions for her house and property. I don't need any money from my mom and she had always wanted to leave her estate to charity, which I supported. I can't get into the details of it right now, but I think my mom's changes had something to do with protecting her property from being sold to developers, like the Good Life Realty Company."

"And she hadn't told you anything about this?" Emily asked.

"No, I'm sure she didn't want to worry me. Plus, she'd made the changes right before she died. I'm sure she would have filled me in when she thought the timing was right. Mom and I told each other everything, but I know she would often omit things if she thought I would worry about her. I tried to get her to move to California many times over the past few years, but she always reminded me Coral Shores was her home, so I stopped asking. I think that was when my mom started filtering what she told me. If there was something to worry about, I'd probably start pushing her to move out here again."

"Well, you can't second guess yourself now. Your mom was a strong and independent woman, and that's something to be celebrated."

"You're right. We will honor her life with a beautiful ceremony. I may fly back in the next day or two, depending on what happens with this research. I'd love to say hi to you and Elvis, if that's possible?"

"Anytime, Sarah. Let me know when you make your plans."

"Thanks. I'll be in touch. Give Elvis a hug for me," Sarah said, as she ended the call.

All the tiny fragmented facts and details about Mrs. Klein's death were swirling around in Emily's head. Nothing came in to focus and it was giving her a headache trying to sort through it all. A good night's sleep would provide her some clarity. In the morning, a phone call to Duncan could help shed light on what was happening with the investigation. They needed to sort this out, and fast.

CHAPTER ELEVEN

"What?" Anthony exclaimed in disbelief as Emily filled him in on the latest development in Mrs. Klein's case. The news about the poison in the orange juice distracted him from pushing her for details about her date with Mike—at least for the time being.

"I know. It's hard to comprehend. Duncan's phone went to voicemail this morning, but I'm hoping he calls with an update," Emily said as she got Elvis settled in her office.

"We have a jam-packed schedule today, and your first appointment is already here," Anthony said. "Do you want to have dinner together so we can hash over all these facts? It might take me all day to digest this news."

"Yeah. My head was spinning last night, trying to sort it all out. It'll be better if we can talk it through. We might know more by then, too."

"And don't think I've forgotten about your date," Anthony reminded her on his way out the door. "But we can save that for later." Emily rolled her eyes at Anthony, but in return, he gave her a nod and a look that clearly communicated she was duty bound to share the particulars.

Anthony wasn't joking about the busy appointment schedule. Emily worked through her lunch break, but took a minute to check the week ahead to see which day looked the most promising to leave the hospital on time for her second date with Mike. So far, Wednesday was the winner.

Emily had finished entering notes into a patient file when Anthony walked into her office. "The last client is gone and the doors are locked. Do you want to pick up some takeout on your way home? I'm almost done with the staff schedule for next month and will be leaving in a few minutes."

"Sounds like a plan," Emily said. "I'm starving. How about Italian tonight? That new place right before the causeway advertises authentic New York-style pizza. I've heard good things about it."

"Sure, you pick the toppings. I'm good with anything except anchovies and pineapple."

Emily pinched her lips together to suppress a grin. Anthony's pizza aversions had not changed since high school, but he always reminded her, just in case. After placing their takeout order, she leashed Elvis and headed for the door, shouting back over her shoulder, "Oh, and I still have ice cream sandwiches left over from the kids." Anthony replied with a thumbs up.

■ ■ ■

The pizza place had an outdoor order and pickup window, catering to the people riding their bikes to and from the beach. Her order wasn't ready yet, so Emily sat down at one of the nearby picnic tables to check her phone messages. Elvis was content to hang out underneath the table while sniffing around for crumbs.

The first message was from Mike, letting her know he had a great time on Saturday night and was looking forward to seeing her this week. Emily smiled and her heart started racing at the sound of his voice. The second message from Duncan had the opposite effect. It was short and curt. He acknowledged receiving her call this morning, but declined to leave any further information. She wouldn't let him off the hook that easily, but it could wait until she got home.

It felt good being forced to sit still with nothing to do, even if it was only for a few minutes. The sound of the gulls circling overhead, combined with the lingering scent of suntan lotion, was a not-so-subtle reminder that she was fortunate to live near the ocean. Emily's mind was drifting off when the growling noise coming from underneath the picnic table startled her.

"Elvis?" Emily glanced under the table and was shocked to see him baring his teeth. His hackles were standing straight up, giving the appearance of a mohawk hairstyle. He had the uncanny ability to transform himself from a lovable terrier to an attack dog. After scanning back and forth to see if there was another dog approaching their table, Emily gasped when she saw Bucky standing at the pizza takeout window. Their picnic table was at least thirty feet away, but her instincts kicked in as she tightened her grip on Elvis's leash. She was hoping the little terrier would keep his cool and Bucky would leave before seeing them. False hopes, of course, when Elvis started barking in between his growls.

Bucky spun around. As soon as he recognized them, his face became serious and then menacing. Thank goodness she was in a public place because that look alone was threatening. With his pizza in one hand, he used his free hand to form his fist into the shape of a gun and took aim at Elvis. Emily jumped to her feet in a defiant stance to let Bucky know he could not intimidate her. He then made a quick about-face, turning to walk to his truck. Looking over his shoulder a few times, he glared at Emily, as if challenging her to follow him.

If Emily's heart wasn't already racing while thinking about Mike, it was pounding out of her chest after her encounter with Bucky. Elvis continued to growl until the delivery man's truck was out of sight. Emily had always considered herself to be an even-tempered person. It's not that she was a pushover or never lost her cool, but the rage she felt right now was foreign territory. Her fury was all-consuming until the repeated call of her name from the pickup window brought her back into the moment. Knowing Anthony would be there soon, she was eager to return to the safety of her own home. They now had one more thing to talk about.

The moment Emily walked through the doorway; it was obvious from the look on her face that something was wrong. Anthony had been petting Bella, but set her down on her cat tree and walked across the room to meet them.

"It happened again—Bucky and Elvis had another run-in."

"Are you okay?" Anthony asked.

"We're fine. Elvis knew Bucky was standing nearby before I did. This time Bucky sort of threatened us," Emily said as she formed a gun with her hand, demonstrating his actions.

"He actually did that?"

Emily nodded her head in defeat. "We need to think this through. Maybe Bucky really hates dogs and Elvis picks up on that or there's a bigger connection between Mrs. Klein, Bucky and Elvis's instincts."

"I'm with you. It has to mean something."

"Let's eat first. I'm so hungry, and I need a minute to unwind. I won't be able to think straight until I have something in my stomach."

"Here, Em. I have a glass of iced tea poured for you and plates on the counter. Let's go outside and decompress," Anthony said.

"Wise man," Emily said with gratitude. "Thank you."

They sat together in silence while inhaling their New York pizza, which they agreed was a new favorite takeout spot. After dinner, Emily leaned her head back on the chaise lounge, closed her eyes, and tried to clear her mind. When she sat up and looked around, Anthony was grinning at her.

"It's like I could see your brain churning away," he said.

"It might be churning, but I don't feel like I'm getting any closer to understanding the significance of all these recent events."

"So, do you want to fill me in on your date first or talk about the investigation?"

"Investigation. I thought if we could go over everything that's happened this past week, my questions for Duncan may be more coherent." Anthony nodded his agreement to the plan.

It took them over an hour to dissect every single detail, starting with their original house call to Mrs. Klein and ending with Elvis and Bucky at the pizza place tonight. They both were big fans of detective TV shows, so while channeling their inner Sherlock Holmes, they tried to break it down by means, motive and opportunity. At least that's the way every other TV detective worked a case.

Determining the means was the easy part, since they knew the poison was in the orange juice. Mrs. Klein would have ingested it without being aware of the danger. Emily couldn't accept the fact that sweet Mr. Bengle was involved in something like this, but she forced herself to leave his name on the list of suspects.

"What about motive? She was the kindest lady, so it's hard to imagine that someone would intentionally do her harm," Anthony said.

"The Good Life Realty Company had been trying to get her to sell her huge oceanfront property. I think she had one of the largest lots in the area. Money is always an excellent motive."

"But would someone resort to murder over a real estate deal?" Anthony asked.

"Maybe they didn't intend to kill her," Emily said, frustrated there wasn't an obvious or plausible motive for her death.

Anthony's face crinkled up while thinking about who could do something like this. "Anyone from town would know about her heavy smoking habit. Do you think the choice of nicotine as the poison was an attempt to hide the source? Nobody would be shocked to find nicotine in her system."

"Who knows," Emily said. "That sounds like a question for a medical examiner or a toxicologist. Maybe they didn't know she was a smoker, and it was the combination of nicotine from her cigarettes and whatever was in the juice that created the lethal dose."

"That leaves us with opportunity. It's possible they put the poison into the orange juice container anytime between packaging, stocking the shelves at the store, and delivery to Mrs. Klein. Maybe it was a random act and not meant specifically for her?"

Emily moved her head from side to side in disagreement. "I don't buy that. I don't like coincidences, and it's no coincidence that Mrs. Klein was a heavy smoker who ended up being poisoned with nicotine."

"We should get one of those big crime boards they use on detective shows so we can display all the facts, complete with photos of our suspects. I bet Duncan and your handsome detective have one," Anthony said.

"You need to stop calling him that. You'll jinx it," Emily said, smiling.

"So, I guess that means you had a good time?"

"It was great. He's so charming and funny. You already know how handsome he is, so what can I say? We're going out again this week."

"That's great, Em. I'm so happy for you."

"Thanks, Anthony. I'm happy for me too."

"Speaking of dates. If you're okay here, I'm going to pass on the ice cream and head home. I told Marc I'd go for a bike ride with him after dinner."

"Sure, I'm good. I need to call Mike, Duncan and Sarah Klein tonight before it's too late. Let's hope I'll have more info to add to our means, motive and opportunity lists by tomorrow."

"If this keeps up, I'm going to buy a big, white, dry erase board we can use for our crime board. We need one in my office anyway, so we can repurpose it after we catch the killer," Anthony said.

"I don't think Mike or Duncan would appreciate you referring to when *we* catch the killer. The message I'm getting from both of them is crystal clear. Stay out of it."

"And are you? Going to stay out of it, I mean," Anthony asked.

"Nope. I feel I owe it to Elvis, Sarah and Mrs. Klein."

"Please be careful. I'm getting a bad feeling about this Bucky guy," Anthony said as he grabbed his keys.

"I will. Promise."

Anthony used his own key to lock the door behind him while Emily sat quietly, contemplating her next steps. Recapping all the details of Mrs. Klein's case with Anthony renewed Emily's sense of urgency about solving this senseless crime. Time to make some calls.

Sarah Klein answered on the first ring. "I'm so glad you called, Emily."

"Is everything okay?"

"Yes, it's been a big day. A lot has happened. Do you have a few minutes?"

"Of course. What's up?"

"Well, your brother and Detective Lane have been very busy. They've approached Mr. Bengle about getting fingerprints from all of his staff at the grocery store, to see if any of them are a match for a partial fingerprint they found on mom's juice container. Mr. Bengle was happy to cooperate, but some of his employees were pushing back and refused to volunteer their prints. They were told it was just for exclusion, but some of them weren't buying it."

"Let me guess—was Bucky one of them? He was that delivery guy I told you about. The one that Elvis doesn't like."

"I don't know, but it wouldn't surprise me. The orange juice container was covered in my mom's prints, but there was a single unidentified partial print on the edge of the lid. They had no luck matching the fingerprint they lifted to any that are already in the system. The plan is to start with everyone from Bengle's and if they don't find a match, they'll pursue other leads. If they can't get everyone's prints, the next step is to get a court order for those who refuse."

"Sarah, I had a question I was hoping you could help me with. It's about the nicotine poisoning. Was there any chance it was the combination of your mom's smoking and the addition of the nicotine in the juice that caused her death?"

"The levels in her system were so high it would have been lethal, even if she was a nonsmoker."

"Oh, I'm sorry. I'm sure this is hard to talk about."

"It is, but at least things are moving along now. You beat me to it, but I was going to call you tonight to let you know that I'm planning to fly back to Florida before the end of the week. I'm going to meet with mom's lawyer about the estate, and I feel compelled to be near the investigation. My need for closure is the primary motivation for my trip, but to be completely honest, I'm a bit of a control freak. If I'm there, I think I'll be able to force the outcome somehow. It's illogical, but being so far away has been difficult."

"It makes sense to me. Let me know when you have the details worked out. We can get together for that beach walk with Elvis. He'd love to see you."

"Seeing Elvis will be the boost that I need. Thank you, Emily. I'll be in touch."

"Well, that's interesting," Emily said to herself after hanging up. Finding a match for the fingerprint would allow them to haul someone in for questioning.

Emily struck out twice, trying to reach both Mike and then Duncan. She left a message for Mike to let him know that Wednesday night would be great for a date night, and she even offered to cook dinner. It was her turn to check the turtle nests, and she thought he would enjoy that.

Emily hoped Duncan wasn't purposefully avoiding her calls. She knew he struggled to keep secrets from her, and maybe ditching her calls was the easiest way to keep her out of the case. It would not work, even if she had to show up at his house to force a conversation. Emily thought it might be a good idea to suggest Mac and Ava come over for dinner tomorrow so they could visit with Elvis. If she could get Duncan here with Jane, he would have no choice but to talk to her. As soon as her plan materialized, she firmed up the timing in a quick phone call to Jane. They would all be there for dinner and sunset tomorrow night. Mac got on the phone to tell her he was happy she was keeping her pinky swear promise for their playdate with Elvis. "Auntie Em, you're the best!"

Emily needed to reconfigure her appointment schedule so she could get home in time to host this impromptu family night. She did not know what to cook for dinner, even if she had the time to prepare something after work. Suddenly, a perfect plan came into focus. Bengle's market sold prepared gourmet meals that were available for order and delivery. Emily wasn't excited about the chance of seeing Bucky again, but thought it could provide a solution to a potential problem. What if Bucky was one of the hold-outs who refused to volunteer his fingerprints to the police? Emily could fill in that missing piece of the puzzle. What could she order from Bengle's that might guarantee an excellent set of Bucky's fingerprints? A case of water! It's wrapped in plastic and he would carry it without a grocery bag. Emily opposed buying single use plastic water bottles, but not this time. If she could get Bucky to carry the case into the house, she could preserve his prints for Duncan and Mike to process.

She wished she had that big crime board on her wall with all the pertinent details, so she could add a drawing of a case of water under Bucky's name. Who knows if this was even legal, but she didn't care. Ordering water and having it delivered was legal, even if her motives were more diabolical.

After logging on to Bengle's website, she chose a family-sized meal of baked ziti and a side of cheesy garlic bread. She picked the largest and therefore the heaviest case of water she could add to the delivery. If Bucky had to wrap both his hands around the case, it upped her chances of getting a good print. She would have him set the case in the pantry for her so she could avoid touching it. She watched enough TV to know it was important to avoid contaminating the evidence. The only glitch would be if someone other than Bucky made the delivery. She'd have to take that chance.

Emily was proud of her master plan. Under normal circumstances, she would share her ideas with Anthony, but keeping it from him this time was for his own good. He would worry about her investigating on her own. Bucky could be a loose cannon, and Emily knew she had to be careful.

CHAPTER TWELVE

When Emily arrived at the veterinary hospital the following morning, she found Anthony in his office, already immersed in the day's work.

"Morning. Could you call Mrs. Betancourt to see if she can come in earlier with Fandango to recheck his skin infection, even over my lunch break, if necessary?" Emily asked. "I need to leave a few minutes before closing time."

"Sure," Anthony said, even though it wasn't like Emily to leave early. "Did you move up your date with Mike?"

"No. Jane, Duncan and the kids are coming for dinner. Mac and Ava made me promise they could see Elvis again, and I thought this would be a good way to corner Duncan. He's not returning my calls."

"Oh, I get it. It has less to do with Elvis and the kids and everything to do with the murder case. I'm on board. Give me a minute while I call Mrs. Betancourt." Anthony walked to the front desk to consult with Abigail, the receptionist. Fandango Betancourt was currently the last scheduled appointment of the day, but Mrs. Betancourt was retired and usually quite flexible, as long as it didn't interfere with Fandango's meal times.

Emily was unsure if she should tell Anthony about her plan to get Bucky's fingerprints. Deep down, she knew she was taking a risk by orchestrating another meeting with the surly delivery man. She didn't want Anthony to talk her out of it, but it would be impossible to hide anything from him. She'd be as successful at that deception as Duncan was at keeping things from her.

It had always been that way ever since they were kids. Duncan was the worst liar, always giving himself away. It's probably what made him such an outstanding police officer. His truthfulness and integrity were defining personality traits. Likewise, Anthony had an uncanny ability to read Emily's little cues, so he always knew what she was thinking, even when she was avoiding the truth. While she was still mulling it over, Anthony returned with the good news that Mrs. Betancourt preferred coming in for her appointment tomorrow morning. Emily decided that honesty was the best policy.

"Before you say anything, I have to tell you I already have my plan in motion."

Anthony sat down at his desk before asking, "What are you talking about?"

"Sarah Klein told me the police found a partial fingerprint on Mrs. Klein's orange juice container, and they're gathering prints from everyone who works at Bengle's in order to eliminate them as suspects. But, a few of the employees aren't cooperating. While I'm only guessing, it wouldn't surprise me if Bucky was on that list of *uncooperatives*. I've ordered a delivery from Bengle's for tonight's dinner and added a large case of water to the order. Hopefully, he's the one making the delivery and leaves behind a treasure trove of fingerprints on the plastic wrap that covers the water."

Emily sat staring at Anthony, waiting for his objections, but he just sat there, staring back at her. After what seemed like minutes, but was less than ten seconds, Anthony's shoulders fell limp in defeat and he let out an enormous sigh. "Okay. I know I can't change your mind, but there's no way I'm letting that creep show up at your place again without being there with you."

Emily's first instincts were to tell him she would be fine, but then she paused. "Thank you. It could all be a bust if someone other than Bucky makes the delivery, but I already feel better about the plan with you there to back me up."

"I'm not even going to ask if you've run this by Duncan or Mike because I already know the answer. Are you even sure this is legal?"

"It's not illegal since it's just a grocery order. I'm not one hundred percent sure if the police can use the prints with that whole evidence-chain-of-custody issue, but if they can't, maybe Sarah Klein's private pathologist can use them. And no, I haven't talked to her about it either. She'll be in town near the end of the week, and we've planned to get together so she can see Elvis. I'll talk with her when I see her, depending on how things play out."

"When is the delivery scheduled to arrive?"

Emily interpreted his request for details as a sign he was now on board with her plan. A good thing, since she was going to do it with or without him.

"Between six and seven o'clock. Duncan and Jane will be there right after seven with the kids. Do you want to stay for dinner? Marc is welcome to join us, too."

"I'm in, but I think Marc has a work thing tonight. I'll double check. Now, I've got a ton to do so we can both leave early. Let me find out if Abigail can close up for us tonight."

Emily was fortunate that Abigail, the head receptionist, stayed on after she bought the hospital from Dr. Dinsmore. She was a valuable member of the team and pivotal to Emily's success. Celebrating with a client after adopting a new family member was easy. It was much harder to provide comfort to a family after losing their beloved cat or dog. Abigail was skilled at doing both and always knew what to say.

There was something so pure about the relationship people had with their pets and supporting that bond was Emily's primary responsibility. Veterinary school prepared her for the medical and surgical skills she needed to be a good vet, but the intangible knowledge that would make her a great vet came with time and experience. A lifelong pursuit.

Emily had walked halfway out of Anthony's office before she spun around to face him. "Why would there only be one partial fingerprint on the orange juice container? I mean, other than Mrs. Klein's. Multiple people handled that container during shipping from the supplier and then again when it was unloaded and stocked at Bengle's."

"Someone must have tried to wipe it clean of prints, but they missed a spot."

"Exactly! It sure points to a planned crime."

"I think they call that premeditated." Emily was impressed with Anthony's use of the technical term.

"Right. Someone got sloppy and left behind a clue. Let's hope it points to the killer."

Anthony had a solemn look on his face when he nodded in agreement. The reality of the violence of the crime in this otherwise safe and sleepy town weighed heavily on them both. They were so focused on the details of the case; it was easy to lose sight of the big picture. A sweet old lady had been murdered. Emily picked Elvis up in her arms, hugged him tight, and moved to her office to get her day started.

Emily worked with efficiency through a morning of routine appointments. It meant she had enough time during her lunch hour to make her monthly trip to the accountant to deliver and discuss the hospital financials. Cutler and Cutler Accountants had been helpful in guiding Emily through the purchase of the veterinary hospital, and she appreciated their ongoing business advice.

The accounting office was conveniently located in a small, three-story building, only ten-minutes from the hospital, which gave Emily enough time to eat her lunch during the drive over. As she pulled into the parking lot, she was aware for the first time the Good Life Realty Company also had their offices in the same building. Their logo was on the top of the street sign at the curb. Funny, she hadn't noticed it before, but since she didn't need the services of a realtor, it must have flown below the radar.

Emily was gathering up her documents when, out of the corner of her eye, she saw Bucky leaving through the front door of the building, walking straight for his pickup truck. It was hard to tell if he recognized her or not. He slowed down while glancing back in her direction a couple of times. Emily ducked down in the seat to hide from him, then got miffed with herself since she shouldn't have to hide from anyone, let alone Bucky. Maybe it was her instincts telling her to be careful.

"I'm sure it's a coincidence," Emily muttered under her breath. Since she didn't actually believe in coincidences, her senses were on high alert as she got out of the car. Inside the front entrance, there was a board listing the businesses in the building. The Good Life Realty Company appeared to occupy the entire third floor. Other than her accountant, the other tenants included; an OBGYN, pediatrician, European travel agency and a chiropractor. Emily took a deductive leap and ruled out the first two possibilities, but she needed to know for sure.

She walked into the travel agency and asked the receptionist if someone fitting Bucky's description had been there. She lied and said he was her brother and she was supposed to pick him up, but he wasn't answering his phone. The travel company representative, and then the chiropractor, both confirmed that nobody who looked like Bucky had been in today. To be certain, the friendly receptionist at her accountant's office told her the same. By process of elimination, Bucky had visited the Good Life Realty Company. Maybe he was buying some real estate, or maybe he was up to no good? If Emily had to guess, it would be the latter. It was tempting to go into the realtor's office after a quick meeting with her accountant, but her lunch hour was up, and she had to rush to get back to the veterinary hospital in time for afternoon appointments. She might consider pursuing a visit in the future, but only after thinking it through.

Focused on finishing her day early, Emily postponed telling Anthony about Bucky until their dinner tonight. Duncan also needed to know about her last few interactions with the Bengle's delivery man. She thought it could inspire Duncan to share with her in return—a quid pro quo over some pertinent facts in the case.

"Okay, you two. If you're going to get out of here early, better go while the coast is clear," Abigail said as she walked into Anthony's office, where Emily was sitting with Elvis.

"Thanks, Abigail. We're leaving now," Emily said. "But if an urgent case comes in, we can turn around. See you tomorrow."

. . .

Her mood during the short drive home was quiet and somber. Emily was feeling anxious about her plan and the possibility they were inviting danger into her house. She had to assume Anthony felt the same way.

"I feel bad that I've dragged you into this," Emily said to Anthony as they both walked from their cars to the front door of the cottage.

"You haven't dragged me anywhere. We're in this together, Em. I know we're outside our comfort zone, but I feel we need to keep pushing forward. For Mrs. Klein and Elvis."

"And for Sarah."

Emily went to freshen up and change while Anthony fed Elvis and Bella. After they'd eaten, Bella walked over to Elvis, sniffed his face and gave him one quick lick on his ear before returning to her cat tree. It was the closest thing to a show of affection between the two of them so far.

"I think she's warming up to him," Anthony said to Emily as she came into the kitchen.

"Maybe. I still think she's mad at me for bringing him home. I'm going to set the outdoor table for dinner. Can you keep watch for the delivery truck? Elvis needs to be locked in the bedroom before we answer the door."

"Sure. I can also hold on to Elvis instead. We could test to see if he responds the same way to Bucky again."

"I want Bucky to feel comfortable enough to carry the water into the house so I can avoid having to touch it. He won't do that with Elvis snarling at him."

"True."

As Emily finished setting up for dinner, Anthony informed her that *Operation Fingerprint* was in motion when he saw the delivery van pull up, with Bucky driving. He picked Elvis up and closed him in the bedroom.

"Yes! I love it when a plan works out. Okay, let's be cool. I don't want him to think anything is weird," Emily said.

"I'm going to stay around the corner in the kitchen so I can hear what's going on. I don't want Bucky to see me. He might say something to you he wouldn't say if I were standing there."

Emily's confidence was bolstered by having Anthony here for backup. It was at this moment she realized how threatened she felt by the delivery man. Maybe her imagination was getting the better of her, but Emily never regretted trusting her gut instincts.

There was a loud knock at the door before Bucky hollered, "Bengle's delivery. Make sure that dog of yours is locked up."

Emily opened the door and struggled to hide her disdain for the man. "He's not a dangerous dog, you know."

"Whatever you say, lady. Where do you want the groceries?"

"I'll take the food, but please set the case of water down right over there, on the floor of the hall closet." Emily had already opened the closet door so that it would be obvious where she wanted it placed.

As she set the groceries on the kitchen counter, Elvis started barking and growling from the bedroom. Anthony whispered, "Do you want me to get him?"

"No. Let's wait until Bucky leaves."

"Are you sure that mutt is locked up?" Bucky called out from the front entry.

Anthony followed Emily back to the front door and stood next to her with his arms crossed and his legs locked in a wide stance. Bucky needed to know that Emily wasn't always home alone, just in case. The delivery man appeared startled to see him standing there.

"I told you he was secure," Emily said.

"He never reacts that way with anyone else," Anthony said. "Elvis was previously owned by an older lady who lived nearby on the beach. I think you made grocery deliveries to her house, too. Mrs. Klein? She died last week."

"I don't know what you're talking about, but that dog attacked me here on a delivery."

Emily was about to reply when Bucky said, "Whatever," and walked back to his delivery van. He couldn't get out of there fast enough.

"What a charmer," Anthony said after closing the door. "Did you see the look on his face when I mentioned Mrs. Klein? If I had to guess, that's what panic looks like."

"You should have told me you were going to say all that about Mrs. Klein."

"I'm sorry, Em. I didn't plan it. He was just so rude about Elvis. I don't like that guy."

"Same," Emily said before releasing Elvis from lock-up.

It took Elvis fifteen minutes to calm down again after patrolling around the door. He sniffed the case of water sitting on the floor until Emily closed the hall closet to keep him from slobbering on the evidence.

A few minutes later, Duncan and Jane arrived with the kids. Elvis was the first one to greet them, inundating Mac and Ava with dog kisses, which resulted in squeals of joy and laughter. Only the aroma from the ziti could distract the kids from playing with him.

After dinner, Jane and Emily were in the kitchen putting the food away when Emily decided now was the best time to speak privately with Duncan. She needed Jane's help to make it happen. "I want to ask Duncan a few questions about Mrs. Klein's murder, but I don't want the kids to hear us talking. Would you mind taking them and Elvis for a short walk on the beach?"

"Sure, Em, but you know your brother. If it's about the case, he won't say much."

"I know, but I have some stuff to tell him too," Emily said.

Jane nodded, then called out, "Kids, let's take Elvis for a walk."

"Yay!" was the echo back.

"Can I hold his leash?" Mac asked.

"Me too," said Ava.

"Sure, we can all take turns. Let's go," Jane said while directing the kids toward the beach.

Duncan was visibly uncomfortable. His attempts to avoid her over the past couple of days had come to an abrupt end.

"I want to fill you in on a few things that have happened with Elvis and Mrs. Klein's case this week, and I didn't want the kids to hear." Emily sat back down at the table.

"Em, you know I can't talk about this."

"I know, but Anthony and I have both witnessed what I'm about to tell you. We think it's important."

After describing all the interactions between Bucky and Elvis, she told him they knew about the partial fingerprint on the orange juice container. Duncan sat there, expressionless, listening to it all. It wasn't until Emily reported seeing Bucky leave the Good Life Realty Company earlier that day that he stood and walked to the kitchen, grabbing a beer from the fridge. He took a swig and paced back and forth in front of the table. Emily knew he was wrestling with what he could or would divulge to them, but she kept silent. Letting him work through it on his own time was the best strategy since pushing him before he was ready could backfire. She gave Anthony a look that communicated *quiet patience.*

"Emily, you and Anthony need to stay out of this. Please," he said with a stern voice before sitting back down. "Things are breaking open in the investigation, and I don't want you to get in the way, even if it's unintentional. Suspects can become dangerous if they're feeling cornered, and that's when innocent people get hurt."

Duncan's serious tone struck Emily, forcing her to pause while she considered whether to drop the subject. Anthony filled that void when he said, "Duncan, you know your sister. She will not stop trying to figure it out. I can tell you one hundred percent that Elvis's reaction means something. It freaked me out the first time I witnessed it. Have you been able to find out if Bucky was making deliveries to Mrs. Klein before her death?"

Since Emily was stuck in the middle between wanting more input in the case and keeping the peace with her brother, she was thankful Anthony wasn't afraid to ask the obvious questions.

Duncan sat staring at his beer bottle before answering. "Yes, he'd been to her house before."

"Have you been able to get his fingerprints to compare with the juice container?" Emily asked.

"I can't answer that," Duncan replied.

Emily and Anthony looked at each other. Duncan was going to be angry when he heard about tonight's delivery, but they had no choice at this point. Emily avoided making eye contact with her brother until they had finished their story.

"You what?" Duncan slammed his fist on the table and then stood in protest. "What were you thinking? This is police business, and you are now actively interfering with this case."

"Well, I might have done it differently if you'd returned any of my calls. No matter what you say, I am involved in this."

Anthony spoke up right away. "That's also why I'm here tonight. I would never let Emily be alone when Bucky made the delivery. We're being careful."

The look of concern on both Emily and Anthony's faces helped diffuse the situation. These recent events were taking their toll on everyone. Duncan took a deep breath and sat back down at the table, softening his tone when he said, "I know you both want to help, but you need to trust me. There's a lot going on that you don't know about. If it makes you feel better, we are looking into Bucky and whether he played a role in any of this, but please promise me you'll stay away from him."

"Okay, we will. But what about the fingerprints I collected tonight?" Emily asked.

"I can't use those, but I'm sure you knew that. Any evidence needs to be collected lawfully."

Emily was about to object when Jane and the kids came bounding into the cottage with Elvis. Duncan seized the moment to make his escape and avoid any further probing questions from Emily and Anthony. "Kids, tell Auntie Em and Mr. Anthony, thank you for dinner. It's time to go."

"Awwww. Please, Dad. Can we play with Elvis a little longer?" Mac asked, pleading for more time.

"I'm sorry, kids. It's a school night, and we've got to get home. I'm sure you can come and see Elvis again real soon. Right, Em?"

"Auntie Em, can we come again on the weekend?" Mac asked.

"Sure, as long as it's okay with your mom and dad," Emily said while Anthony sat grinning from the periphery of the negotiation.

Jane tried to appease the kids with a compromise. "We can visit Elvis on Sunday, but that means you need to say good night. Give Auntie Em and Elvis a hug and then we're going home. Deal?"

"Deal, Mommy," Ava said.

Duncan was holding the door open and once the kids and Jane were out of earshot in the front yard, he turned to Emily and Anthony. "I'm not kidding around about you staying out of this. For both your safety and the integrity of this investigation, you'll stand down. Got it?" Before they could reply, he was gone.

Anthony locked the front door and turned to Emily. "Ouch. Duncan is so angry. That's the only time I can remember him losing his temper, even if it was for a fleeting moment. I can't blame him, though. You know he's worried about you, right?"

Emily nodded. "I get it. I'll be cautious, but I'm not going to stop searching for answers."

"Will you make me a promise?" Anthony asked, his tone making it clear he wanted Emily to understand the serious nature of his request. "No more rogue operations. You need to keep me in the loop and guarantee me you won't do anything on your own without backup."

"I promise," Emily replied. Anthony took her at her word and they both agreed it was a good time to call it a night.

CHAPTER THIRTEEN

It wasn't a conscious decision to back off after Duncan's reprimand, but throughout the next day at work, Emily didn't think about the case, or Bucky. Her patients and the hospital were all-consuming. She put her head down, working hard so she could leave early for her date with Mike. Her hectic pace meant she didn't have a chance to get nervous about the evening ahead, despite Anthony constantly reminding her that tonight was a big deal.

"It's just a second date," she told him.

"I get that, but when was the last time you had a second date?" Anthony asked. Since she could not answer his question, he had made his point. "Are you going to talk to Mike about Bucky's fingerprints sitting in your front hall closet?"

"After Duncan's reaction, I'm not sure. I'll wait to see if the topic comes up," Emily said with a shrug.

When Emily left the hospital, Anthony was busy discharging Muffin and Mittens Clark—today's dental surgery patients. Emily understood it was nerve-racking for pet owners who often sat by the phone waiting to hear that everything was okay after a procedure, so she always made a point to call her clients right away. Anthony was tasked with ensuring Mrs. Clark understood the post-op instructions.

Without enough time to prepare a nice dinner for Mike, Emily stopped at Kings Seafood on her way home to pick up their ready-to-grill shrimp kabobs, delicious sides of Bahamian peas and rice and coleslaw. Add in a couple slices of coconut cake, and she now had a delicious homemade meal—at least homemade by someone.

Elvis appeared unimpressed that his post-dinner beach walk was shorter than usual in order to give Emily time to freshen up before Mike arrived. She was certain that if a dog could sulk, this is what it would look like. He was staring out the patio doors when Bella came and sat down beside him. That's interesting, thought Emily. Friends at last?

She was scrambling to finish putting on some mascara and lip gloss when she heard a knock at the door. "I'll be right there." Having run out of time to do anything with her hair, she opted for a ponytail.

"Hi Mike. Come on in." He greeted her with a quick kiss on the lips before Elvis commandeered all his attention.

"Hey, Elvis," Mike said, while obliging him with a belly rub. "How was your day at the hospital?"

"Me or Elvis?" Emily replied jokingly. "We both had a busy day, but that's normal."

"Same here, but I'm officially off-duty and excited about seeing another turtle hatch tonight," Mike said.

Emily was smitten. Smart, handsome, funny and an animal lover—Mike was the real deal.

"I was about to start the grill for dinner. Hope you like shrimp kabobs?"

"I love all seafood and can handle the grill for you."

"Sure, thanks." *And he can cook.*

Mike was outside, carefully monitoring the shrimp while Emily finished setting out the rest of their dinner. After bringing him a cold beer, she sat down on the chaise lounge, sipped her glass of wine, and took a few deep breaths. It was the first time she had relaxed all day. Mike glanced over at her, grinning.

"What?" Emily asked.

"I don't know. I was thinking about how much my life has changed this past year, and for the better. In the beginning, I was looking for a new start, but it's shocking how fast Coral Shores now feels like home, as if I've lived here forever. I'm glad I met you, Dr. Emily Benton."

Emily knew she was blushing, but didn't care. "I'm glad too," she replied, once again feeling tongue-tied. How lame, she thought to herself before changing the subject. "Duncan told me you lost your dad a couple of years ago. I'm really sorry. I know how hard that is."

"Thanks. He'd been sick for a long time before he passed away."

"Duncan also mentioned your mom recently moved to Florida. Do you get to see her very often?"

"Between my work and her busy social schedule, it's been hard. She seems so happy and is making a bunch of new friends. Her retirement village offers every activity you can think of."

Emily stopped short of asking more personal questions since Mike was removing the shrimp from the grill, signaling it was time for dinner. After a delicious meal over light-hearted conversation, they agreed to save dessert for later so they could get to the turtle nests on time.

"I'm not sure we'll see a hatch tonight, but it could be any day," Emily said as they were walking up the beach, holding hands.

"It's great just being out here. I've been working with a realtor to find a place close to the water. I'm hoping to see a few prospects this weekend."

Emily was doing back flips on the inside. "Let me know if you need my help. I can give you the inside scoop on potential locations."

Mike pointed ahead. "Aren't those your turtle friends, Marlon and Sharon?"

"That's them. They beat me here tonight. I hope everything is okay," Emily said while picking up her pace.

Marlon was the first person to welcome Mike back to the watch. When Sharon joined them, Emily noticed her nudging Marlon in the ribs with her elbow. She was grinning as she looked back and forth between Emily and Mike. There was no doubt the turtle volunteers were supportive of Emily's new relationship.

"Have we missed anything?" Emily asked while scanning the nearby nests for signs of activity.

"I don't think tonight's the night," Marlon said as he bent down to straighten the wooden stakes supporting the rope barricades. "But it will be soon for these two nests here."

"Did I get my schedule mixed up?" Emily asked.

"No, it's your turn," Sharon said. "We were going for dinner and thought we'd stop for a quick check. We're brainstorming ideas for the Coral Shores Turtle Project Fundraiser that's scheduled for next month."

"Can we count on you to be there, Mike?" Marlon asked.

"Sure. I'd love to help if you have any jobs for newcomers." Sharon was still grinning at Mike, while glancing back at Emily. She was not very subtle.

"I'm sure there will be lots of opportunities for you to get involved. Well, we'll leave you to it then. Thanks again for coming out, Mike," Marlon said, as he and Sharon began walking toward the parking lot.

"I think they have a crush on you," Emily said.

"They're just happy to have a new volunteer in their midst. This is an enormous commitment."

"I guess, but taking a walk down the beach doesn't seem like much of a hardship," Emily said with a smile.

This evening's volunteer watch ranked as Emily's favorite of all time, despite the absence of baby turtles. As they wandered from nest to nest, while holding hands, they shared stories about their lives. Mike was attentive and funny. It was long after sunset when they started walking back to Emily's cottage. She had planned to probe Mike for details about Mrs. Klein's case, but needed to be subtle in her approach. It had been a wonderful second date, and she didn't want to mess everything up.

"I was wondering if Duncan filled you in on all my encounters with the Bengle's delivery man, Bucky?"

"Yes. He also told me you attempted to illegally collect some evidence."

"Well, I wouldn't say that ordering a case of water is illegal. I assumed Bucky was a holdout on giving up his fingerprints and thought I could help." Emily was annoyed with herself for sounding defensive. She was trying to assist with the case, and it was frustrating to be sidelined.

"You know how dangerous that was? Don't you?" Mike was still holding her hand, but stopped walking before turning her to face him. "There are a lot of things going on with this case that you don't know about, and I can't tell you about. Duncan can't either. Please stay out of it."

"I respect you both and would do nothing to jeopardize the investigation. It was never my choice to be wrapped up in this case. That's why I don't understand why you can't trust me."

"Emily, if anything happened to you, I'd never forgive myself."

The intensity of his plea caused her to pause for a second before asking, "I'm assuming you haven't been able to get Bucky's prints yet, so why can't you collect them from my case of water? Anthony was here that night. He can testify to the fact Bucky handled the case. Doesn't that help with the chain of custody?"

Choosing not to answer her, Mike turned to walk up the beach. That uncomfortable silence lasted until they arrived back at Emily's cottage. The mood of the evening had changed, and not in a good, romantic kind of way. While she regretted pushing him on the topic, she was equally frustrated by his lack of transparency. It was obvious they were both feeling conflicted, and Emily didn't see a way to turn it around in time to salvage the rest of the date. Elvis and Bella's demands for attention lightened the mood, but Mike declined his slice of coconut cake, stating he was still full from dinner and had to get home since he had an early start tomorrow. He gave Emily another quick kiss as he was leaving, but not the passionate embrace she was hoping for.

Emily was muttering under her breath as she closed the door. Bella and Elvis stared back at her with a befuddled look on their faces. "I really think I blew it," she said. Her two furry roommates had nothing to offer in the way of advice but were happy to cozy up on the couch while she ate her slice of cake. It didn't taste as good eating it alone but was comforting nonetheless.

. . .

After waking the following morning, Emily read a late-night text from Sarah Klein. She was arriving in Coral Shores this afternoon and was hoping to schedule a visit with Elvis. Emily messaged her back right away. Sarah was welcome to come over this evening, and they were both looking forward to seeing her again. This news helped brightened her otherwise foul mood.

. . .

Emily arrived at the hospital before Anthony, but it wasn't long after when he came waltzing into her office with a big grin on his face.

"So?" It was obvious he was looking for the juicy details of her date.

"So," Emily said, and then paused. "Not good. It wouldn't surprise me if I never hear from Mike Lane again."

"What? How did that happen? Oh, wait, it was about the fingerprints, wasn't it?" Emily gave him one of those looks that communicated, *obviously*.

"I pushed too hard. Mike gave me a lecture, same as Duncan, so I still don't know what's going on with the case."

"They're only looking out for you, you know," Anthony said.

"I guess. Mike said he couldn't forgive himself if anything happened to me."

"Oh, he'll call again," Anthony said in a confident tone. "Maybe you should let it go for your own safety," he suggested. "At least for a few days."

"We'll see. Sarah Klein is flying in today and plans to stop by tonight to see Elvis. I'm sure she'll have some details to share with me, and maybe it'll help shed some light on the investigation."

Anthony shook his head before saying, "You're a stubborn lady, but I'm here to support you. You need to keep your promise that you won't take any actions on your own, or I'll call Duncan and Mike myself."

"Okay, okay. Let's drop it for now. Kensington is coming in this morning to recheck his kidney values, and I'm hoping for good news. Mrs. Martinez thinks he's back to his old self."

"That would be great news," Anthony said before moving to his office to start his day.

People are very intuitive about their own pets. All the little subtle cues and behaviors they pick up on are very accurate. Emily had learned to trust a client when they say, "she's not quite herself" or "he's back to normal." Kensington's kidney values were back in the normal range. Treating his kidney infection had turned things around and for now, he would stay on his prescription kidney food and recheck again in a couple weeks. Mrs. Martinez was shedding tears of joy after receiving the news. She was hugging Anthony and Emily and the receptionist on her way out with Kensington, thanking them repeatedly for the wonderful care. Kensington even had a spring in his step today.

From that point on, the day was smooth sailing. Emily was in that sweet spot as a veterinarian where she was on schedule with her appointments, surgeries were routine, and she caught up on phone and email messages. During the break right after lunch, there was even enough time to run a quick errand.

"I'm going to pick up some documents from the accountant. I'll be back before my next appointment," Emily said, informing Anthony as she was heading out the door.

"Are you sure you don't want me to get them for you?"

"No, I could use the fresh air." If she was being fully transparent, Emily would have admitted her plan to make a quick stop at the Good Life Realty Company. Duncan and Mike's cone of silence was forcing her to fill in the gaps of information on her own. She didn't consider this to be going rogue since it was a busy office with lots of employees during daytime hours. What could go wrong?

. . .

Emily made a quick dash into the Cutler and Cutler accounting firm to pick up her documents before walking upstairs to the Good Life offices. During her drive over, she decided to tell anyone who approached that she was interested in the properties for sale along the beach. If they probed further, she was going to lie and say she was considering putting her cottage up for sale and was curious about the current market trends. There was no detailed master plan. She wanted to get a peek inside the office, to get a feel for the business.

The receptionist greeted Emily with a friendly smile before asking if she had an appointment. After explaining the reason for her visit, the receptionist left her desk to determine if there was a realtor who could meet with her. While she waited, Emily surveyed all the local properties for sale that were professionally displayed on the wall of the main foyer.

She had only been scanning the listings for a few minutes when loud voices could be heard coming from the back corner office. Two men were arguing about something. Returning to her desk, the receptionist appeared both startled and uncomfortable with the outburst.

"Is everything okay?" Emily asked.

"I'm sure. It's likely a simple misunderstanding." Even though it was obvious from her expression, she didn't believe it.

One voice grew louder, but Emily couldn't make out what they were talking about. Whatever it was, it wasn't good.

"I'm sorry, but none of our realtors are available to meet with you right now. If you could leave me your contact information, someone will be in touch to set up an appointment." The receptionist was struggling to maintain her professionalism since the ongoing altercation was growing louder.

Emily stepped into the hallway that led to the back offices while attempting to eavesdrop on the argument. Suddenly, the door to the corner office flew open, and Bucky came storming out.

"You better sort it out." Bucky turned, growling his warning at the man who had stepped into the doorway behind him.

"Crap," Emily muttered under her breath. There was no way he could get out of the building without seeing her, no matter how small she tried to make herself. The only place to hide was under the receptionist's desk—obviously not an option. She must have looked like a deer in the headlights. Once he was within ten feet of her, she could see he was blind with rage, but not blind enough to overlook her standing there. He stopped dead in his tracks and stared. Unable to predict what was going to happen next, she moved closer to the receptionist's desk to get out of his pathway.

Bucky surprised her when he turned and looked back at the corner office. The man standing in the doorway was none other than Mr. Good Life himself, looking dapper in his high-priced suit. Emily didn't know his name, but he must be the owner of the company because she'd seen his face plastered all over the advertising billboards and benches around town. In an instant, Bucky had gone from looking angry to confused. He turned back to Emily, pointed his finger at her, then marched past on his way out. Mr. Good Life had closed his office door, so Emily could no longer gauge his reaction.

"I'm so sorry about that. That never happens here," the receptionist said, while smiling and trying to make light of the situation. "If I can get your contact info, someone will call you."

"I don't think so," Emily said as she turned to leave. The stairway landing, located outside the main office door, faced a large window that provided an unobstructed view of the street. From her viewpoint, Emily could see a portion of the parking lot and the main road in front of the complex. Until she was certain Bucky was gone, she would stay put. There was no way she was going to walk to her car alone. After waiting only a few minutes, Bucky's blue pickup truck squealed its tires as it pulled out on the road. Emily tightened her purse to her chest and made a beeline for her car, locking her doors as soon as she sat down.

She was almost back to the veterinary hospital when she became aware she was hyperventilating. "Breathe, Emily. Breathe," she said to herself to calm her nerves. Understanding the meaning of what she'd witnessed would have to wait until the adrenalin coursing through her body subsided. Until then, putting together a coherent thought would be impossible. It would have been easier if she had heard what Bucky and Mr. Good Life were arguing about. Once she was safely back at the hospital, her top priority was to research the owner of the real estate company in order to confirm the identity of Mr. Good Life.

CHAPTER FOURTEEN

"Welcome back, Dr. Benton." Abigail greeted Emily as she made her way to her office from the employee entrance of the hospital. "Anthony wanted me to tell you he's meeting with our pharmacy distributor right now; in case you need them for anything."

"Thanks, Abigail. I'm sure Anthony has everything covered." It was a relief he couldn't see her right now, since she needed a few minutes to compose herself. For the first time since finding Mrs. Klein, she was frightened. Someone had made the decision that killing a sweet, retired piano teacher was necessary to accomplish their evil end-goal, whatever that might be. That same person wouldn't hesitate to go after anyone else. Had she put Anthony or Elvis in harm's way? Maybe Duncan and Mike were right. Should she stop pushing so hard to be included in solving the case, since it was clear there were forces at play that she didn't understand? Now was the time to be clearheaded before taking any future action.

Sophia, the eight-year-old Blue Point Himalayan cat, distracted Emily from thinking about her trip to the Good Life office. Sophia's vomiting had started yesterday; she would not eat or drink and was now lethargic. Her abdomen was painful during her physical exam, and a quick check under Sophia's tongue revealed a strand of gold thread. Cats love to play with thread and yarn, and if they swallow a piece, it can get wrapped around the base of their tongue leading to an intestinal obstruction. The loose ends pass along the digestive tract while the string stays anchored at the tongue. It almost always results in an emergency abdominal surgery to relieve the string foreign body.

Sophia's owner, Mrs. Rattary, admitted that Sophia loved to play in her quilting room when she was working on a project. The x-rays confirmed Sophia's obstruction, but by cutting the thread, it was possible she could pass the string, avoiding a major surgery. Her blood work was stable, so she was hydrated with fluids and given medicine to treat her nausea and discomfort. Under a light sedation, the base of the string was cut, releasing the ends into her intestinal tract. Mrs. Rattary had an appointment to bring Sophia back in the morning for a follow-up x-ray and directions to return to the emergency hospital overnight if she continued to vomit.

"Dr. Benton, Sophia will never have access to my sewing supplies again. I promise. Who knew it could be so dangerous? She was having so much fun playing."

"Most people are unaware of this risk to cats. The important thing is you have a plan to protect her from now on. We'll see you tomorrow morning," Emily said, trying to console the worried and guilt-ridden owner.

"We'll be here right when you open. Thank you again," she said before leaving the exam room.

Managing Sophia's case while juggling her afternoon appointments meant she missed a call from Sarah Klein. Sarah was planning to come by at seven o'clock, if it worked for Emily's schedule. Emily texted her back that the timing was perfect.

It was the end of the day before Emily connected with Anthony.

"Wow, we've both had a busy day. I heard about Sophia. Fingers crossed the string passes with no complications," Anthony said as he sat down in Emily's office.

"Yeah, fingers crossed," she said, sounding disengaged as she turned back to her paperwork.

Anthony was staring at Emily. It wasn't like her to be detached from one of her cases, and she knew Anthony could tell that something was up.

"I'm taking Elvis home now. Would you be able to come over right after work? I want to talk to you about something that happened today."

"Em, you're scaring me."

"I'm okay. I don't want to talk about it here. Sarah Klein is coming over this evening, but I need some help to process a few things before she arrives."

"I'll be right behind you. Lock the doors when you get home. Okay?"

"I will. See you soon. And, thanks, Anthony, for always being there." Emily gave him a weak smile before hooking Elvis up to his leash and retreating out the back door.

■ ■ ■

After stepping into her cottage, Emily took exaggerated deep breaths in a feeble attempt to erase the stress of her day. This was her safe place, and she needed that right now. Bella and Elvis did their best to force her out of her own head space—at least for long enough to feed them. The leftover ziti in the fridge was the ideal comfort food, otherwise it would have been a bowl of cereal for dinner tonight. Emily had little appetite, still feeling unsettled after her run-in at the Good Life offices. A good detective never believes in coincidences, and there were too many piling up around Bucky.

Anthony used his key to let himself in and even though Emily knew he was only a few minutes behind, it startled her.

"Emily, what happened? I don't think I've ever seen you this rattled." Anthony's concern escalated after seeing Emily's face. She tried to stop the flow of tears but failed miserably. The stress from the past two weeks had been building and now reached a breaking point. She had no choice but to let it out. Anthony propped her up with an arm around her shoulder and guided her to the couch. As soon as she sat down, Emily tightened her body and pulled back from him, feeling both angry and frustrated she'd let the events of the day get to her this way. She was tougher than this.

Shaking her head to physically clear her mind, she wiped her eyes and said, "It was Bucky again."

Anthony leaned back before scrunching up his face and crossing his arms. "You promised me, Em. I can't protect you if you won't talk to me about what you're up to."

"Okay, but I don't need you to protect me, and it wasn't like that. I didn't plan it. After picking up the accounting paperwork, I went into the lobby of The Good Life Realty office to get a first impression of the place—you know? I mean, it was only up a flight of stairs."

Anthony's face flushed, making it hard to tell if he was angry, or worried, or both. Before he could scold her again, Emily filled the awkward moment with more information.

"After I walked into the lobby, I could hear an argument coming from one of the corner offices. It was impossible to make out what they were saying. I tried moving closer, and that's when Bucky came charging out of the office like an angry bull, leaving Mr. Good Life standing in the doorway. There was nowhere for me to hide. Bucky stopped in his tracks when he saw me and sort of pointed at me before looking back at Mr. Good Life." Emily was mimicking Bucky's threatening, pointing motion for effect. "He then seemed more confused before he took off for the parking lot. The whole thing was horrible and weird at the same time."

"What do you mean by Mr. Good Life?"

"You know, the guy with his face all over the billboards, park benches and grocery cart advertisers. I assumed he's the owner."

"And you didn't hear what they were yelling about?"

"Nope, nothing. It was pretty heated, though. Bucky sort of threatened him as he was leaving. Something like, *you better fix it.* Wait, he told Mr. Good Life, *you better sort it out.*"

They both sat with their own thoughts for a moment before Anthony chimed in. "First, I don't believe for a minute you decided on the spur of the moment to visit that realtor's office. You had already decided before you left the hospital. Am I right?"

"I'm sorry, Anthony. You're right. I should have told you, but I thought it would be a quick and safe outing. I promise never to hide anything from you again. Never. Double pinky swear promise," Emily said, while offering her little finger as a gesture of authenticity.

"Okay, but two strikes and you're out. If you investigate on your own again, I'm calling Duncan."

"Promise." Emily agreed as Anthony offered his pinky finger to seal the deal.

"Second. What the hell is going on here?" he asked. "You know, any good TV detective follows the money. I think we need to follow the money too. Real estate money, that is."

"That's exactly what I was thinking. We need to get some more info on Mr. Good Life. I was about to research him online. Want to join me over some leftover ziti?"

"You know it," he replied as they both moved to the kitchen table to sit side-by-side in front of Emily's laptop while dinner was warming in the oven.

"Mr. Good Life's name is Richard Brant, but there doesn't seem to be much detail on him. He showed up here a few years ago as the Good Life Realty Company, but nothing before that," Emily said and then leaned back in her chair while pondering this information. "Maybe he was in a different line of work?"

"Maybe, but he's building those gigantic beach mansions, so he has to be pretty wealthy. You'd think he'd even turn up in the odd charity fundraiser photo. We know he enjoys plastering pictures of his face everywhere."

"I should tell Duncan and Mike about it today. They're going to be so mad at me, but they need to know. I'm sure with their resources, they'll be able to do a proper background check on Mr. Brant."

"If they haven't already. I can go with you when you tell them. It might help diffuse the situation," Anthony said, offering his support.

"Thanks, but that's okay. I'm a big girl and can deal with whatever comes next. Even if it leaves my dating life in ruins."

Anthony reached for Emily's hand in a show of solidarity. "Hang in there. I'm going to stick around until Sarah Klein gets here and then I'll dash out. I want to meet her, and I don't think you should be alone right now."

Emily squeezed his hand back then held on for a few seconds longer. Anthony was her rock, her best friend, and she appreciated him for being here.

As they finished eating their leftover ziti, there was a knock at the door. Anthony scrambled to put the dishes away so Emily could turn her attention to Elvis, who knew it was Sarah before he saw her. He ran to the door with his tail wagging, ears forward, breaking into uncontrolled spins of joy. Sarah matched his enthusiasm when Elvis jumped into her arms as soon as she leaned down to pet him.

"Oh, Elvis. You are the bravest, sweetest boy!" Sarah exclaimed, while being inundated with dog kisses.

"He's so happy to see you. He doesn't even get that excited when my niece and nephew come to play with him." Emily said, smiling.

"I don't believe that for a minute. Elvis loves kids and they love him back."

"Sarah, this is my best friend, Anthony. He's also my hospital manager and has been helping me take care of Elvis."

"It's nice to meet you, Anthony. Thank you from the bottom of my heart for watching out for Elvis."

"I'm really sorry about your mom. She was my piano teacher when I was a kid. I was glad I got to see her again with Emily just before," and then Anthony's voice trailed off.

"It's okay, Anthony. It's hard to talk about, but since you knew my mom, you know she would want us to keep fighting for the truth," Sarah said.

"That's for sure." Anthony nodded in agreement. "I was about to head out. Enjoy your beach time with Elvis. Em, I'll see you tomorrow." As he was walking out the door, he motioned Emily to call him later, which she confirmed with a subtle nod.

"Sarah, I have a few things to tell you and thought we could talk while walking Elvis. It's a gorgeous night to catch the sunset," Emily said.

"Sounds good. Let's go, Elvis."

Emily shared the good news first. Elvis was off all his medicine, and so far, there had been no relapse of his cough. Sarah beamed with joy. The bad news came when Emily described her run-ins with Bucky, the realty company visit, and Elvis's repeated reactions to the delivery man. Sarah didn't say anything until after Emily finished telling her about Bucky's fingerprints that were still sitting in her front hall closet.

"That's fantastic, Emily. I understand why your brother couldn't accept them as evidence, but I can still have them analyzed. If you don't mind, I'm going to call my forensic specialist to see if someone can come straight away to collect the prints for processing."

Emily's mouth must have been hanging open, leaving Sarah with the impression she may have overstepped until Emily added, "They can come anytime. I'm so glad we can test them to see if they're a match to the print from your mom's orange juice container."

Sarah stepped away to make her call, and when she rejoined Emily and Elvis, she was smiling. "Someone will be here in the next hour or two to pick up the case of water. Thank you, Emily. You took a significant risk trying to get the prints, and with everything else you've told me; I'm worried about you. Maybe it's time you left it to the professionals. In this situation, I agree with your brother and Detective Lane."

"Trouble has come looking for me and Elvis, not the other way around."

Sarah was quiet for a moment before sharing the most important news of the evening. "Your instincts about the Good Life Realty Company are spot on. It's always bothered me how they were escalating their tactics and threats toward my mom to get her to sell her property. My investigative team has turned up some interesting information about the owner, Richard Brant. I don't want to say too much since it's now in the hands of law enforcement."

"I knew it. It's exactly like Anthony said—follow the money. I wonder what Brant's connection is to Bucky."

"I think this delivery guy may be the missing link. Maybe these prints will fill in the pieces of the puzzle."

"I sure hope so," Emily said.

Diffusing Elvis of his sandpiper-chasing energy took longer than normal tonight, so the sun was setting when they turned to make their way back to Emily's cottage. Sarah wanted to wait until the forensic technicians picked up the fingerprint evidence, and Emily was happy to have the company. It was hard to admit she was still feeling uneasy after running into Bucky today.

Sarah's private forensic team arrived within the hour. She greeted them in the driveway before Emily showed them the case of water sitting in her closet. They were wearing protective gear and gloves so as not to contaminate the evidence, and then it was carefully loaded into their van. Emily was given an official receipt for the evidence before they departed for the lab.

"How soon will you know the results?" Emily asked.

"I'm sure they'll have the analysis done in the morning," Sarah said. "If it's not a match, then we can leave it to the police as they pursue other suspects. If it is a match, it will complicate things, since we can't use this evidence in a court of law. Emily, you've taken tremendous risks to help bring my mom's murderer to justice, and I'm indebted to you for the loving home you've given Elvis." Sarah started to tear up before walking over to pick Elvis up into her arms. "You mentioned Elvis loves spending time with your niece and nephew. Is there any chance your brother and his wife would reconsider adopting him?"

Emily thought about it for a moment before replying. "I'm not sure. Every time I see Duncan, we end up butting heads about the investigation, so the topic hasn't come up. I can talk with my sister-in-law, Jane, to see what she thinks. Mac and Ava sure love Elvis. They're constantly planning their next play session with him."

"I don't want to put any more pressure on your family. You've already done so much, but to see Elvis in a home with kids would bring me such joy."

"I agree. He's amazing with them."

Sarah put Elvis back on the floor and went to grab her purse before saying, "I'm not sure how long I'm going to be in town this time. Your fingerprint evidence might change everything. Are you okay if I come and see Elvis again before I leave?"

"Absolutely. You're welcome here anytime," Emily replied.

Sarah gave her new friend a hug, pet Elvis once more, and then walked out of the cottage. Emily could tell it was difficult for Sarah to say goodbye to Elvis each time she left. He was an integral part of all her recent memories of her mom, and it was impossible to separate the two.

Emily was standing in the front yard, holding Elvis and waving goodbye to Sarah, when she noticed a pickup truck parked a few houses down the street. It matched the general description of Bucky's blue truck. The setting sun made it difficult to see the details, but from this distance, the truck looked empty. Elvis was due for a short walk, so she could perform double-duty while checking it out. Emily knew most of her neighbors and couldn't remember seeing a blue truck in any of their driveways. It was probably nothing to worry about, but she wouldn't be able to rest until she knew for sure.

Emily was fifty feet away from the truck when Elvis started with a low-pitched growl and pulled at the end of his leash. She could see better now, and despite confirming that no one was sitting inside, Elvis's reaction caused Emily to stop in her tracks. She started to panic the moment he began snarling and barking. Bucky sat up straight in the driver's seat. He must have been leaning over to hide. Their eyes met for a second before he started the engine, put it in drive, and squealed the tires as he accelerated toward Emily and Elvis. She only had seconds to get Elvis off the road and onto the front lawn of her neighbor's house before Bucky swerved, missing them by only a few inches. Emily was paralyzed with fear, trying to decide if she should knock on her neighbor's door to escape inside for safety or pick Elvis up and run as fast as she could back to her own house.

Bucky drove past Emily's cottage and was halfway to the next intersection when he slammed on his brakes. He sat idling in the middle of the road for less than a minute. To Emily, it felt like an eternity. She held Elvis as tight as he would allow, waiting to see what Bucky would do. A quick scan of her neighbors' properties confirmed no one was out in their yard. While planning her next move, Bucky took off again, heading south down the beach road. When he was far enough away and no longer posed an imminent threat, she sprinted home. Emily ran inside, slammed the door shut, double checking that all the doors and windows were locked. She'd been putting off telling Duncan about her visit to the Good Life Realty Company, but now she had no choice. She was scared and needed her brother's help.

CHAPTER FIFTEEN

"Come on, Duncan. Pick up." Emily had called Duncan's cell phone over and over and he wasn't answering, causing her irrational mind to take over. Had their relationship deteriorated to such a low point that he was avoiding her calls? She was getting desperate and needed to track him down.

"Hi, Em. What's up?"

"Jane, is Duncan with you?"

"Sort of. We're at Mac's baseball game and Duncan is on the field coaching. It's wrapping up now, and the kids are having their post-game team huddle and popsicles. Why?"

"Can you walk over to him and ask him to call me right away? It's important." Emily peeked through the front curtains to confirm Bucky was nowhere in sight.

"Em, are you okay?"

Not wanting to scare Jane, and knowing Ava was sitting next to her watching Mac's game, Emily tried to tone down the panic in her voice. "I'm okay, really. I just need to speak with him."

"He's finishing now. I'll give him the message and make sure he calls you."

"Right away—before he leaves the park," Emily reiterated.

"I will, but now I'm worried. Are you sure you're all right?"

Emily took a deep breath before answering. "I promise I'm fine, and I'll fill you in later."

"I'm packing up my chairs and stuff, and I'll get him the message in a minute. Call me back if you need anything."

"Thanks, Jane."

Emily sat there, tapping her fingers on the side table, staring at her phone. She contemplated dialing 911 but had faith that Duncan would call, and he did.

"Em, what's the rush? Jane said it was urgent," Duncan asked.

"I need you to come right away. Bucky, that delivery guy, tried to run Elvis and me over on the road."

"What! Are you okay? Where are you?"

"I'm at home and we're fine, but I'm a little freaked out. A few things have happened today that I need to tell you about. Can you come?"

"I'm with Mac's baseball team, and I need to wait until all the kid's parents come and pick them up. It shouldn't be long—maybe ten minutes. I'm sending an officer to your house, but I want you to stay on the phone with Jane until they get there. Okay?"

"Okay, and then you'll come when you're done?" Emily was feeling vulnerable, which was uncharted territory for her. Duncan must have been able to sense it in her tone.

"Em, I'll be there as fast as humanly possible. I'm hanging up now so Jane can call you. Are your doors locked?"

"Yes, and thanks, Duncan. Please hurry."

As soon as Emily hung up, Jane called. It was impossible to avoid updating her on everything that had happened over the past couple days, but Jane could only offer brief replies since she was trying hard to avoid alarming Mac and Ava, who were sitting in the back seat of the car. They'd been talking for less than ten minutes when Emily heard a car pull into her driveway and could see the flashing police lights through her drapes. She looked out the window to confirm the cavalry had arrived and gasped in relief when she saw Mike get out of his car.

"Jane, Mike's here. I'm okay now, and I'll talk to you later," she said before hanging up the phone.

After the awkward end to their date last night, Emily wasn't sure what to expect. As soon as Mike walked through the door, all the tension fell away. He held her in a long embrace before backing away, just far enough so he could see her face. She was trying to hide the look of fear that had consumed her since the moment Elvis started growling at Bucky's truck, but she wasn't doing a very good job of it.

"Are you okay? Is Elvis okay?" Mike asked as he wrapped his arm around Emily and led her over to a chair, glancing around for Elvis, who was busy chewing on his favorite bone near the patio doors.

"We're fine. Maybe shaken up a little. How did you get here so fast?"

"When Duncan called me, I was only a few miles up the beach with my real estate agent looking at a townhouse."

"Oh." Emily was thankful he was close by, but somewhat surprised he had looked for a new place to live without including her in the search. She thought he would at least consult her about the location first.

She must have done a poor job of hiding her disappointment, prompting Mike to say, "My realtor called today about a brand-new listing that hasn't hit the market yet. I had to move fast." Emily nodded, but said nothing.

Mike looked down to read a text. "Duncan is only a few minutes away. It's probably best if you wait until he gets here to tell us what happened, so you don't have to say it twice."

"Makes sense," Emily said as she relaxed, just a little. Having Mike in her cottage was the main reason, but she was also shifting from the flight response of her latest Bucky run-in to the fight response. She was getting angry that he was once again threatening her.

Mike stood and walked toward the kitchen. "Do you want something to drink?"

"I'll take a glass of wine. Whatever's open in the kitchen is fine. Thanks, Mike."

He poured her a glass and grabbed a bottle of iced tea for himself before suggesting they go outside on the deck. Listening to the calming sound of the waves as they broke onshore was the perfect antidote for Emily's difficult day.

They hadn't been sitting for long when Duncan came storming through the door, still wearing his baseball uniform. He rushed to Emily's side and gave her a once over to check for injuries.

"Duncan, I'm fine. Really." Emily said, reassuring him while also relieved the recent tension between them seemed inconsequential right now. Convinced she was okay, Duncan sat down and exhaled.

"We need to stop getting together like this. Em, I swear I've aged ten years in the past two weeks from worrying about you."

"I'm sorry. I'm not doing it on purpose. Most of the time, anyway," Emily said, keenly aware she had gone into the Good Life Realty office today on an unsanctioned reconnaissance mission.

"What do you mean by *most of the time*?" Duncan asked.

"Can I get you a beer? Something else to drink?" Emily asked while moving toward the kitchen, stalling while deciding how to reply to his question.

Duncan grabbed her hand, guiding her to sit back down. "I'm fine. Take your time, Em, and tell us everything that happened."

Since both Mike and Duncan were aware of all her previous run-ins with Bucky, she only had to fill them in on her trip to the real estate office, her conversation with Sarah Klein, the forensic techs who picked up Bucky's fingerprints, and that Bucky had been watching her place tonight before trying to run her over. They were listening in their official role as law enforcement officers, serious and intent on getting all the details. They interrupted her a few times, to ask a question or two, in order to clarify parts of her story. When she finished, they all sat in silence, digesting the information.

"I think I'll take that beer now," Duncan said, as he stood and walked to the kitchen. "Does anyone else need a drink?"

Both Emily and Mike simultaneously answered, "Yes," their shared laughter lightening the mood.

Before Duncan returned to the patio, Mike jumped to his feet, addressing the urgent topic at hand. "Actually, I'll pass on that beer. We need to get an arrest warrant issued for Bucky. We didn't have enough probable cause until this attempted hit-and-run tonight, but at least now we'll be able to get his fingerprints." Mike confirmed Bucky was the holdout from Bengle's who had refused to volunteer his prints.

"I knew it," Emily said.

"Did any of your neighbors see him attempt to run you over?" Duncan asked.

"No. I looked around to see if anyone was outside, just in case I needed a safe haven." Emily paused before adding, "A few of my neighbors have those video doorbell systems. Maybe they have security cameras, too."

"We'll check with them since any corroborating evidence will help us keep Bucky in custody," Mike said. "I'm going to make a few calls to get the ball rolling."

"Em, can you walk down the street with me and show me where he was parked and approximately where he almost hit you?" Duncan asked.

"Sure. Let me grab Elvis's leash so he can have his last walk of the night," and then she paused. "I just realized something. When Sarah Klein's technicians were here, Bucky likely saw them loading the case of water into their van. The van had the company logo on the outside, so he had to know that something was up."

Mike and Duncan looked at each other. More than ever, there was a sense of urgency to get Bucky off the street. If he was feeling cornered, he might continue to act in an erratic and dangerous way.

Bucky had no prior arrests and until this case, he was unknown to the police. That didn't mean he wasn't capable of violence. Emily felt good to be part of the team, at last. She understood all the reasons they were shielding her from the investigation, but it was frustrating to be kept in the dark.

"I'll walk Elvis," Duncan offered, as they were heading out the front door. As Emily handed him the leash, it reminded her of the conversation with Sarah Klein about whether Duncan and Jane would be interested in adopting Elvis. She decided now was not the time to broach the subject. They had only passed by the first neighbor's house when he said, "Elvis is great at walking on a leash, isn't he?"

"Yup, he always comes when he's called when he's off his leash, too."

"Em, we have a long night ahead. Could you call Anthony to come and stay with you? I'm also going to have an officer patrolling the area—at least until Bucky is in cuffs."

"I owe Anthony a call, anyway. He's always there for me, and he made me promise I wouldn't investigate on my own anymore."

"At least one of you has some common sense." Duncan was grinning when he gave his sister a gentle nudge with his shoulder.

"I know, I know. I promise to leave the police work up to you and Mike from now on," Emily said before adding, "But I've been thinking about my run-in with Bucky at the real estate office this afternoon. His facial expression when he first saw me was more confusion than anger. He turned back toward Richard Brant as if he was trying to figure out why I would be there. From the way Bucky was threatening him, I wonder if he was feeling cornered or trapped. Maybe he was worried he was being set up to take the fall. That's assuming he's guilty of doing something illegal."

"Maybe," Duncan said. "It's the only explanation for why he showed up tonight to intimidate or hurt you. Somehow, he's figured out you're involved in all of this."

Emily stopped to show Duncan where she first saw Bucky's truck and then where he swerved when Emily and Elvis jumped off the road to avoid being hit. Duncan noted all the houses that were in visual range of the street so he could direct the police officers that would begin their canvas for video surveillance of the incident. As soon as they were back in the cottage, Emily called Anthony to enlist his help once again. He was heading out the door before she even hung up.

Mike pulled Duncan aside for a private conversation before turning back to Emily. "I'll try to check in on you tonight, but I'm not sure if it will be too late," Mike said as he prepared to leave. "Duncan told me that Anthony is on his way. Will you promise to stay inside with the doors locked? There will be officers nearby while they check with your neighbors for video evidence, but we'll also have a car patrolling the area through the night."

"I'll probably be awake until I hear from you that Bucky is behind bars. Come by or call anytime," Emily said, aware that Duncan was watching her with that brotherly grin on his face. He could tease her without saying a word.

After Mike left, Duncan and Emily stayed inside to wait for Anthony. Elvis took only a moment to jump up on the couch beside Duncan, who then started petting the terrier's ears.

"No pressure, but Sarah Klein asked me tonight if you and Jane would consider adopting Elvis. I told her how much fun he had playing with Mac and Ava." Emily held her breath, waiting for his response.

Duncan looked down at Elvis, who was swooning from his ear massage. "I hadn't really thought about it. Elvis is the only thing that Mac and Ava talk about lately. Maybe?"

"Really?" Emily replied with a little too much enthusiasm.

"After Jane's dog, Scooby, died, she wasn't ready to adopt another dog right away. Then along came Mac and Ava and it seems like life was so busy, with my long work hours, Jane finishing grad school and all their activities. I guess they're getting to the age where they could help take care of Elvis, especially since he's so good at walking on a leash."

"I was nervous about bringing it up tonight with so much stuff going on. Why don't you talk to Jane about it when you can? Elvis will be with me until you decide either way." Emily thought it would be wise to avoid putting any pressure on him.

"Okay, maybe. Let's not mention it to the kids until Jane and I have a chance to think it through."

"Sure. And if it helps, I can always pet sit for Elvis when you need. I actually think Bella is growing fond of him, and he's fun to have around." Emily was grinning from ear to ear at the prospect of keeping Elvis in the family.

Just then, Anthony knocked before letting himself in to the cottage. Emily mustered up all of her energy and greeted him with a little wave.

"Thanks for coming, Anthony. I'll let Emily fill you in on all the details. Will you be able to stay for the night?" Duncan asked as he stood up and grabbed his phone and keys, preparing for a quick exit.

"I ran out the door to get over here, but Marc is packing me a bag and will drop it off later tonight. I can stay for a few days if it comes to that. You okay, Em?"

"I'm better now."

"I'll let you know as soon as I have any news," Duncan said, and then he left to meet Mike at the station.

Anthony looked over at Emily with the most somber expression she had ever seen. "This is bad, isn't it?" he asked.

"I think so." Emily filled him in on all the details of the evening. Anthony was shaking with anger when she told him about the attempted hit and run.

"It has to be him. Bucky delivered groceries to Mrs. Klein and is refusing to volunteer his fingerprints. He's a known associate of this realtor who was threatening her, and now he's coming after you. And to top it all off, Elvis really dislikes him. I'd say Elvis hates him, but my mom told me never to use that word. We should have all been following Elvis's lead from the very beginning."

"I agree that Bucky's guilty, but he doesn't seem like the mastermind criminal. Not based on all our encounters so far. Maybe he got in over his head."

"Maybe, but I don't care. He needs to be behind bars. At least until they can sort it out," Anthony replied. Emily nodded in agreement.

There wasn't much more for them to talk about. They watched some comedy reruns on TV, which was the perfect counterbalance for the serious circumstances in which they had found themselves. In between their binge-watching of episodes, Emily remembered she actually had some good news to share.

"I forgot to tell you. There's a chance that Duncan and Jane might adopt Elvis. I didn't think they were interested at first, but after watching him play with Mac and Ava, Duncan said he would talk to Jane about it."

Anthony picked Elvis up in his arms and whispered in his ear, "You are a lucky man, Elvis."

"Duncan has a lot on his plate right now, so I won't push it, but I'm feeling good about this. It's like Elvis knew he was auditioning for his forever home tonight when he snuggled up beside Duncan. And you should have seen him walking on his leash tonight—as if he was in the show ring."

"Wise man," Anthony said. Elvis stared at the two of them before jumping off the couch to attend to his chew bone that he'd abandoned when Anthony arrived. Bella had moved down a few levels on her cat tree, inching closer to Elvis. It was either a show of affection or an interim move as part of an impending ambush. Bella still wasn't happy she had to share her house with him, but appeared to accept the reality he was there to stay.

"I'm not planning to say anything to Sarah about Elvis yet. Too many other things taking priority right now," Emily said.

"That's an understatement. They have to find Bucky tonight. It's the only way they can get his fingerprints in the legal and official way."

"I should probably tell Sarah about everything that's happened, but I'm sure her techs are already working on the prints they collected from my house. Plus, I promised Duncan I'd stay out of it, for now anyway."

Anthony gave her another one of those looks that clearly communicated his thoughts. "Who's kidding who here? You'll stay out of it as long as it takes to finish that glass of wine."

Emily just shrugged. Tonight, she was content knowing the wheels of justice were turning. For the first time, she felt they were getting closer to the truth about what happened to Mrs. Klein. That knowledge allowed her to let go of the tension of the day, but left her feeling exhausted. Before the next TV commercial break, she was sound asleep on the couch. She felt safe knowing Anthony was here, and a police officer was driving up and down the street. After getting Emily to sleep-walk to her own bed, where she collapsed into a dreamless slumber, Anthony met Marc at the door to collect his luggage. Marc confirmed he would stay on call if they needed anything. Everyone understood the gravity of the situation, and Marc was no exception.

CHAPTER SIXTEEN

When she woke the next morning, Emily was feeling disoriented and had to sit on the edge of the bed to collect her thoughts. Stress and exhaustion were playing with her mind, and it took a moment to piece together all the events from yesterday. She checked her phone, but there were no updates from either Mike or Duncan. What did that mean? Were they still looking for Bucky, or was he being interrogated? Understandably, they had a lot going on and might have been too busy to call, but Emily was frustrated she was not being kept apprised of the investigation like they promised.

It was just after dawn, and the bright, early morning sun was beckoning her outside. Daylight brought a sense of safety that was hard to find in the dark of night. Elvis was dancing in front of her, obviously in need of a potty break.

"Let's go, Elvis," she said while stepping in to the closest pair of flip-flops and grabbing his leash. Anthony was still sleeping, and since she would be back in a few minutes, there was no need to leave a note. Elvis headed straight for the water's edge and expertly patrolled the nearby beach to make sure there were no sandpipers to chase off. While Emily was watching Elvis, she saw his playful gait change in an instant. He had turned to look up the shoreline and was rigidly standing still with his hackles up, and then growled. This time Emily didn't even need to look in the direction he was staring to know what was happening. She scooped him up and started running for her cottage. A quick glance over her shoulder confirmed what she already knew—Bucky was on the beach, running toward them. Emily held Elvis tight and ran faster than she knew she was capable of. She made it onto her deck and through the patio doors before slamming them shut and engaging the locks.

Anthony had been standing in the kitchen, staring at the coffeepot, willing it to work faster, when Emily came crashing through the door. "What the hell, Em?" he said while clutching his chest. "I thought you were still sleeping."

"Bucky's out there and started chasing us. He'll be here any second. I'll call 911 from the home phone, but my cell is on my bed. Go call Duncan and tell him it's an emergency." Emily was shouting out instructions while running around the house, double checking all the locks on the doors and windows. She closed the patio blinds so Bucky could not see into her place and raced to put Elvis and Bella in the guest room, safely out of harm's way.

Anthony ran back into the room with Emily's phone. "Here, Duncan wants to talk to you."

"Duncan, he'll be at my door in seconds," she hollered into the phone.

"I want you to stay out of sight of any windows and don't leave the cottage, no matter what."

"What if he breaks in? What are we going to do? I don't even have a baseball bat. Anthony, go grab those huge kitchen knives in the wood block." Emily knew she was panicking, but this was the best she could do under the circumstances.

"Em, Mike's on the radio with the officer who's been in your neighborhood all night. He's there and he'll handle everything. Don't open the door until I tell you it's safe."

Emily took a deep breath, trying to calm her nerves, but still accepted the large knife Anthony was handing her.

"Can you stay on the phone with me?" she asked.

"I'm here. You're going to be okay. I promise."

Emily nodded to the phone as if Duncan could see her response. She and Anthony had moved into the living room and were sitting on the end of the couch, far away from the windows. She told Duncan he was on speakerphone and set the phone down on the coffee table. While squeezing Anthony's hand, their free hands were each wrapped around the handle of a large knife that neither of them had the skill set to use as a defensive weapon. Suddenly, there was a loud commotion on the patio.

"Freeze! Coral Shores P.D. Put your hands up. Now!" shouted an authoritative voice.

They could hear what sounded like her chaise lounge or the dining table being toppled or pushed around on the deck, and then it was quiet. Anthony and Emily looked at each other and then back in the patio's direction.

"Should we check to see what's going on?" Emily asked, forgetting she was still on the phone with Duncan.

"No. Don't you dare," Duncan yelled in to the phone.

She whispered into the speaker. "What if he needs our help?"

"No," was his only reply, and then she could hear Duncan talking to someone else in the background. Their muffled voices made it impossible for her to understand what they were saying.

"Bucky's cuffed and in custody. Officer Braddock is securing him in his squad car. You're safe now. The officer will stay out on the road until Mike gets there with more back up. It'll only be a few minutes, but stay inside until Mike knocks."

"Yes!" Anthony jumped to his feet, shouting in victory. He was jubilantly waving his big knife over his head. Emily erupted in an uncontrolled laughing fit at the sight. Her reaction seemed so out of place that Anthony stopped dancing long enough for Emily to remove the weapon from his hand.

"Oh," Anthony said. "I didn't even realize I was still holding it." Once they were weapon-free, they hugged, and then Emily joined

Anthony in his celebratory dance. It was irrational, but she had so many raw emotions sitting right at the surface. A silly, ill-timed dance-a-thon seemed the perfect way to release the tension. It was either that, or she was going to crumble onto the floor in a weeping mess.

"Should I let Bella and Elvis out of their bunker?" Anthony asked.

"They're quiet right now. Maybe Bella is helping to keep Elvis calm. In case we end up with people in and out of my place, it's best to leave them in the bedroom."

"Emily." It was Duncan, attempting to get her attention. "Mike is outside your front door, so you can go out now. I'm hanging up, but I'll be there soon."

"Thanks, Duncan. For everything," she said, relieved to feel safe again.

"Yes, thanks, Duncan," Anthony added.

Emily and Anthony went out into the front yard. The flashing lights from three patrol cars illuminated her cottage and the street beyond. Mike appeared to be wrapping up a conversation with an officer, who had turned to walk back to his vehicle. Emily assumed it was Officer Braddock since Bucky was sitting in the back seat, cuffed, shoulders slumped, and with a defeated look on his face. Emily was uncertain, but it almost looked like he was crying. Before she could thank the officer for saving them today, he pulled onto the road heading in the direction of the police station.

Mike turned and walked toward Emily and Anthony. "It's over," he said, reassuring them both before wrapping his arm around Emily's shoulder and pulling her into the safety of his embrace. "Hi, Anthony. Are you doing okay?"

"I'm good now. I made a fresh pot of coffee and I think we could all use a cup," Anthony said. The three of them made their way inside the cottage, where Emily moved to release Bella and Elvis, while Anthony filled the mugs. It was no surprise to anyone that

Elvis charged toward the patio doors, sniffing and then growling at the remnants of Bucky's scent.

"So, what happens now?" Emily asked, while savoring the first sip of her morning pick-me-up.

"That will be up to Bucky. He's going to be charged for your attempted hit and run and now for trespassing and an attempted break-in. If his fingerprints are a match for Mrs. Klein's juice container, he could be facing first-degree murder. He won't be making any deliveries for a very long time."

"I still don't think Bucky is the guy behind the plan. Everything in my gut tells me he's working for someone else."

"Maybe, but we'll need to let the evidence and facts lead the investigation. If Bucky is wise, he'll read the writing on the wall and be willing to offer testimony for consideration of leniency in his sentencing."

"If we're counting on Bucky to do the wise thing, then we may be out of luck," Anthony said.

"I'm always amazed at the survival instincts of any low-level criminal. Bucky will not take the fall for the greater good," Mike said.

Anthony glanced down at his watch and then jumped to his feet. "Em, we have to get to the hospital. It's already eight o'clock, and Mrs. Rattary is likely waiting there with Sophia." Mike looked confused until Anthony clarified. "Sophia is a cat."

"Got it. I'm on my way to the station, but I promise to stop by the hospital when I can with an update."

"Promise, promise?" Emily asked, attempting to hold him to his word.

"Promise," Mike said, giving her a quick kiss on the cheek before letting himself out the front door.

Emily and Anthony didn't have time to dissect their eventful morning. They were too busy scrambling to get to the hospital on time. They rode together to work since Anthony had already stated his intention to return with Emily at the end of their day. Neither one of them knew if the danger was over and until then, Anthony was going to stay close.

. . .

"Good morning, Dr. Benton. I have the best news. Sophia has been eating really well overnight and there's been no more vomiting. She's acting like her normal self again, too." Mrs. Rattary had arrived at the hospital before it opened and was the first person in the lobby after Abigail unlocked the doors.

"That is great news. We're going to repeat Sophia's exam and her x-ray, but based on your update, it sounds like she might have passed the thread without complications. I'll be back with her in a few minutes."

Mrs. Rattary was right. Sophia was bright and perky. Her abdomen was no longer painful on palpation and she appeared to be well hydrated. She was even purring during her checkup. The x-rays confirmed what Emily already knew—Sophia had avoided an emergency surgery.

The rest of the day was busy enough to keep Anthony and Emily from having any time to discuss their morning. That didn't stop Emily from checking her phone every chance she got, hoping to see an update from Mike or Duncan. It wasn't until right before closing time when Duncan sent her a text confirming that Bucky was behind bars. He promised to fill her in later that night and passed along an apology from Mike that he'd been unable to come by the hospital today. There was nothing more she could do for now. Anthony made the executive decision to call ahead with their Indian food takeout order from Curry-in-a-Hurry so they could pick it up on the way to Emily's. The drive home afforded them their first opportunity to talk in private.

"What I wouldn't give to be a fly on the wall in Bucky's interrogation room," Anthony said.

Emily thought about it for a minute before adding, "That would be one way for us to find out what's going on. I've been thinking about it, and I don't understand why a successful realtor would resort to murder to get his hands on a piece of real estate."

"It makes little sense, but we know nothing about this guy. Maybe he made his money the old-fashioned way—through criminal enterprise."

Emily raised her brows at Anthony's suggestion. "Maybe."

After a quick stop to pick up their takeout, they spent the rest of the ride home in silence. Returning to the recent scene of the crime was leaving them with a feeling of dread as they continued to process the events from the past day.

"I'm starving. Do you want to eat first and then take Elvis for a beach walk?" Emily asked while unpacking their dinner containers.

"Yes, food first, for sure. I missed lunch today," Anthony said. "What about you, Elvis? Food first?" The attentive terrier tilted his head to the side, signaling his agreement.

"I'm going to text Duncan to tell him we'll be on the beach in case he's planning to drop by. I don't want to miss the chance to talk to him."

"Does Sarah Klein know about all of this, including Bucky's arrest?"

"I assume so, but I told Duncan I'd stay out of it. Maybe I'll reach out to her to see if she wants to join us for a walk with Elvis tomorrow evening?"

"Good idea. I'll feed Elvis and Bella and you put your plan into motion."

"It's not a plan," Emily said, challenging his assumption she was going to meddle, even though she was already texting Sarah with a proposal to get together.

"Whatever you say," Anthony replied with a grin. Emily rolled her eyes back at him. She knew she was being less than transparent about her true motive of getting some cold, hard facts.

After feeding the furry family members, Emily and Anthony took their takeout on the deck. It was difficult to stop themselves from looking up and down the beach, on alert for any danger. Even though Bucky was in jail, it was impossible to comprehend he was the root cause of all this violence and death. That was the main reason she felt they could not let their guard down just yet.

Anthony was putting the leftovers away in the fridge. "I ate too fast. I think a walk will help me digest."

"Let's go so we can be back before the sun sets," Emily said, and then grabbed Elvis's leash.

"Do you need to check the turtle nests tonight? It's been a long time since I was on a watch—it would be fun."

"No, my next night is on the weekend. Sharon and Marlon are training new volunteers over the next few days."

After walking up the beach for ten minutes, Emily looked out at the horizon and decided it was time to turn back so they could be home and behind locked doors before sunset. She couldn't shake the feeling of déjà vu when she reached the exact location from this morning where Bucky tried to chase her down. She didn't even want to think about what he had intended to do if he'd been able to catch her. Emily was staring out at the ocean when Anthony asked, "Is that Mike?"

Emily turned and smiled when she saw Mike walking toward them, waving his arms. There was no sense of urgency based on his casual gait, so she let out a sigh of relief. Anthony was grinning at her when he said, "Now I feel like a third wheel."

"Not at all. I'm glad he's here, but I don't want you to go. If that's okay with you?"

"I'm not going anywhere. No matter how handsome or charming your boyfriend is."

Emily elbowed Anthony in the side. A gesture to communicate, *no teasing*.

"Duncan told me you were going for a walk. Did you see the turtles tonight?" Mike asked.

"No, we didn't walk that far up the beach," Emily said.

"We wanted to get back before it got dark. I think we're still feeling the residual effects of the last day. Do you have any news for us?" Anthony asked.

"There's been a major development. I can't say much because it's still an active investigation."

"What can you tell us?" Emily asked as they were approaching her patio deck.

"Bucky's working with his court-appointed lawyer on a plea deal for his cooperation and testimony. You'll likely hear it from Sarah Klein, but the fingerprints you collected from the case of water came back as a match to the orange juice container. Her forensic team sent the report over this afternoon. We still can't use them to build a case against Bucky, but that's okay. His prints were collected legally after he was charged with your attempted hit and run."

Emily understood that *Operation Fingerprint* ended up being an academic pursuit. Anthony winked at her while giving her two thumbs up. He was proud of her for taking the initiative, even if it was a risky decision at the time.

"So, I guess that means he wasn't acting alone. Was I right that Mr. Good Life is behind all this?" Emily asked.

Mike paused and thought about it for a minute. "I can't confirm or deny that fact," and then he smiled.

"I knew it," she exclaimed. "But why?"

"That I really can't comment on. Things are moving fast and I wanted to let you know that while I think you're safe now, we're still going to continue with increased patrols around your house tonight."

"I'm okay with that," Anthony said.

"Have you briefed Sarah Klein on everything?" Emily asked.

"Yes, she's fully aware. Her forensic tech team has helped to build the case we have. I can't stay, but I wanted to make sure you were all right after this morning. Are you staying overnight, Anthony?"

"I'll be here tonight, and tomorrow if necessary." Mike shook his hand and asked Emily if she could walk him out to his car. Emily looked over her shoulder at Anthony and shrugged as she followed Mike into the front yard.

"Listen, Em," Mike said, while turning to face her and taking her hands in his. "These last couple of days have been really intense. Despite everything that's going on, I've been thinking about you. You and me."

"You have?"

Mike nodded. "Once this case wraps up, I'd like to plan another date, or a few dates."

"I'd like that too," Emily said. Her heart was racing, and she was sure he could see it beating through her chest. Mike put his arm around her waist with one arm and pulled her toward him, gently brushing the hair off her face with his other hand before kissing her. This time it wasn't a quick peck on the cheek but an intense, lingering kiss. When they pulled apart, they were both breathless.

Mike smiled and shook his head. "Amazing," was all he said before turning to walk to his car. "I'm sure Duncan will be in touch. We'll let you know if anything happens."

Emily didn't even have the words to hold him to his promise. She just smiled and waved as he pulled out of the driveway. After turning around, she could see the front window blinds flutter, giving away Anthony's brotherly surveillance. As she walked into the cottage, Anthony handed her a glass of wine and said, "Today sure ended better than it started."

Emily was still in a romantic haze when she accepted the glass and smiled. "Oh, yeah."

CHAPTER SEVENTEEN

"Em," Anthony whispered. "Emily, it's time to get up."

After jerking to a sitting position, she struggled to shake off the effects of a deep sleep, blinking her eyes as she attempted to focus on the face in front of her. "What time is it? Did I forget to set my alarm?"

"No, it's a few minutes before the alarm. Duncan is on his way. He was texting you, but when you didn't answer, he called me."

"Oh, okay. Maybe he has news for us. Give me a minute, I'll be right out."

"Coffee is on," Anthony said before leaving the room.

Emily was splashing cold water on her face, trying to jumpstart her day, when she heard Duncan's voice. "This can't be a social call," Emily said as she walked into the kitchen to greet her brother.

"Not really, but I always love seeing you, sis." Emily rolled her eyes at that one. "I wanted to tell you before you saw it on the news. Bucky is cooperating with the investigation in exchange for leniency at sentencing. He's being charged for Mrs. Klein's murder based on his fingerprint match to her orange juice container. After first claiming he knew nothing about the poison, he confessed that Richard Brant, of the Good Life Realty Company, hired him and told him the poison would only make her sick enough to end up in the hospital for a few days. We're executing an arrest warrant for Brant, and Mike is at his home right now with a team."

"Really? It's really over?" Emily asked.

Duncan nodded while drinking his coffee. "It's over."

On instinct, Anthony moved toward Emily and put his arm around her shoulders. She could feel the stress escaping her body, leaving her deflated and worried her knees would buckle without all the adrenalin running through her veins.

"How did it all play out?" Anthony asked as he moved to refill everyone's coffee.

"Well, Bucky was refusing to cooperate or say anything until we presented him with the match of his fingerprint to the orange juice container and the evidence of his link to Richard Brant. Payments from Brant to Bucky go back over the past year and a half. As soon as he realized how much trouble he was in, the floodgates opened. Bucky would handle unsavory tasks for Brant. Mrs. Klein wasn't the first person harassed or intimidated in a pressure campaign to get them to sell their property."

"What do you mean?" Emily asked.

"The Good Life Company made their money flipping undervalued waterfront properties and selling them to international and out-of-state investors. Bucky would use vandalism and other threatening tactics to scare residents, tricking them into thinking their neighborhood was becoming unsafe. An all-cash offer was made at the exact moment an owner was feeling most vulnerable. It was too good to turn down."

"That's despicable," Anthony said while shaking his head in disgust.

"We're still trying to piece together the origins of their working relationship, but it appears Bucky escalated his tactics for more money."

"Did he confirm he was the one that broke into Mrs. Klein's cottage?" Emily asked.

"He did. After Mrs. Klein's death, they panicked. Brant hired Bucky to search for any documents and communications connecting her to the realty company. There were threatening letters challenging her property title and setbacks that Brant didn't want coming to light. Bucky didn't say, but I'm assuming he was also going to retrieve the juice container until you surprised him that night, and he fled before the job was done."

Emily was quiet, taking it all in. It overwhelmed her with sadness that Mrs. Klein had lost her life because of someone's greed. It was so cruel and senseless.

"Believe it or not, Bucky blamed his high school math teacher for his current predicament. He actually claimed it wasn't his fault that he got his decimals wrong." Duncan was shaking his head in disbelief. "Apparently, Brant supplied him with the poison and a syringe and needle to inject it into the juice. Bucky got the directions mixed up and ended up dosing her ten times higher than intended. He still doesn't quite understand the repercussions of his actions, eager to blame everyone else."

Emily and Anthony didn't know whether to laugh or cry.

"Maybe that's why he was arguing with Brant the day I ran into him at the real estate office," Emily said.

"Yes, when he realized what happened with the dosing, he confronted Brant. Of course, Brant was blaming Bucky for his carelessness. When he saw you, he was likely feeling cornered as the evidence was piling up around him."

That made sense to Emily after witnessing the end of that encounter. "What about Sarah Klein? Has she been told?"

"Yes, she was our first phone call. The financial forensic team she had on the case identified other potential victims of Brant dating back over two years. They also found many incriminating documents that Mrs. Klein saved to her cloud account. She was a very savvy lady and kept a copy of all her communications with Brant. As far as we can tell, there may be over a dozen people who were coerced into selling their homes because of his tactics. The case will be turned over to the Florida Department of Law Enforcement for further investigation. They can handle crimes that are spread across the state."

"Were there other murders?" Anthony asked.

"Not that we know of. Seems like Mrs. Klein was the first victim to lose her life. Who knows why their M.O. changed, but it wouldn't shock me if Brant and Bucky continue to implicate each other."

"I know firsthand that Bucky could handle any task that required physical intimidation but maybe not the nuanced details of a poisoning. He's not the sharpest tool in the shed. Even if it was accidental and he only thought he was going to make her sick, it's irrelevant now. He needs to pay," Emily said firmly.

"And he will," Duncan said in agreement.

"Does that mean you can now release Mrs. Klein's body to Sarah?" Emily asked.

"Yes, that process is under way, but it will be up to the coroner."

Emily nodded. She knew that having a ceremony to celebrate a loved one's life and passing was an important part of working through the grief and getting some closure. If she had been forced to wait to say a formal goodbye to her mom, it would have been debilitating. Sarah Klein had been so strong.

"I hate to state the obvious, but we've got to get ready for work," Anthony said to Emily as he moved toward the guest bedroom. "I don't think I've ever been so relieved that it's Saturday so we can close at noon. It'll take the entire weekend to catch our breath."

Emily filled her coffee mug for the third time. "Will you let me know what happens today?" she asked Duncan.

"I will. I'm not sure what to expect. Odds are Brant lawyers up right away."

"Of course."

"I want you both to know you should feel safe now. I doubt the judge will grant bail to Bucky, but I'll keep you posted," Duncan said as he set down his mug, preparing to leave. "Oh, and I haven't forgotten our conversation about Elvis. Jane and I haven't talked about it because the kids are always around. Plus, it's been a hectic few days."

"I totally understand." Emily glanced over at Elvis, who sat perched on his favorite pillow on the couch. "Sarah Klein is coming to see him again in the next day or two, so let me know."

Duncan nodded and gave his sister a hug and Elvis an unexpected pet on the head before leaving. Emily moved with purpose; showering and getting ready for work in record time. She took Elvis for a perfunctory leash walk on the street and when she returned, Anthony was packed and ready to go.

. . .

The Coral Shores Veterinary Hospital was buzzing today. An adoption fair, run by the local animal shelter and nearby pet store, had families coming in to schedule health checkups for their new furry family members. Anthony had convinced Emily it would be a good idea to include a free health exam for these rescue pets to support the shelter, create goodwill and build lifelong clients. He was right. The hospital schedule was filling up for the following week and all the new puppies, kittens, cats and dogs had enjoyed some attention and tasty treats from Abigail and the front reception team. A win-win.

"Em, do you want me to stay over again tonight?" Anthony asked as they were getting ready to close the hospital for the day.

"No, I'll be okay now that the bad guys are behind bars. And I've been thinking you should take Monday off too. It's been a while since you had any time off, and it's important to avoid getting burned out. You're my best friend and I worry about you. Plus, you're extremely valuable to the hospital, so we need to keep you healthy."

"What about you, Em? You've been working longer hours than me. When are you going to take a break?"

"I don't know. I knew what I signed up for when I bought the hospital. No illusions of long weekends here."

"Still, it's not healthy."

"I agree, but it's okay for now. The way we've been growing, I think we may need to consider adding another veterinarian soon, even if it's only part time."

"I like how you're thinking. The numbers support it too."

"Until then, I'm keeping my head down. I have some catching up to do after the last couple of weeks, and then I'll consider a break," Emily said.

"Any word from Duncan or Mike today?"

"No, but Sarah Klein sent me a text, and she's coming over tonight to visit and spend some time with Elvis. She's then going back home for a few days before returning for her mom's celebration of life service."

"Let me know if you get any details about the service. We might need to block appointments at the hospital so we can both be there."

"For sure. I'll try to get the details tonight. Thanks again, Anthony. For having my back through everything. I don't think I would have survived the past two weeks without you." Emily's eyes welled up.

"I know you'd do the same for me in a heartbeat. Go home and get some rest. I'll call you tomorrow." Anthony hugged Emily tight before she could see he was tearing up, too.

. . .

After arriving home, Emily changed into her swimsuit and then headed straight for the ocean. A relaxing swim in the Gulf was the perfect way to release the stress and fear that had piled up since Mrs. Klein died. She was floating near the shore, letting the rolling waves lift her up and down, lulling her into a salty trance. Once she was certain the ocean had provided all the healing powers it offered, she rinsed off in the outdoor shower, grabbed a glass of lemonade and brought Elvis and Bella on the patio to join her on her mom's chaise lounge.

What a week. It had been difficult to keep perspective about the danger she was in while it was all happening. Looking back, she realized she was lucky to come out of it unscathed. Anthony, Duncan and Mike got full credit for that, even though she had to admit she'd done a pretty good job of trusting her instincts and following the clues. Actually, it was more about trusting Elvis's instincts. Looking down at the little terrier, she realized he'd been through the biggest trauma of all; losing his forever person, moving to a new home, and struggling to make friends with a gigantic, aloof cat. Emily's thoughts drifted off when a knock at the door brought her back into the moment. She was even more surprised when she opened the door and found Jane and Duncan standing there without the kids.

"Is everything okay?" Emily felt a wave of panic rising inside her since it was so strange to have them over without Mac and Ava.

"Everything is great," Jane replied as they walked into the cottage. "We wanted to talk to you about adopting Elvis without the kids here."

"Oh." Emily assumed they'd come in-person to deliver the bad news that they weren't interested in welcoming Elvis into their family. "I understand."

"What? No, Em. We're here to tell you we'd like to adopt Elvis, but we both wanted to spend some time with him alone, without the kids, to confirm our decision."

Emily was smiling when tears of joy trickled down her face. Jane hugged her, and they walked out to the deck together and found Elvis and Bella sitting side by side on the chair. Elvis was wagging his tail and with each wag, he bumped Bella on her side. Strangely, she didn't seem to mind.

"Hey, little buddy," Duncan said to Elvis before sitting down beside him and petting his head. Jane was more exuberant when she scooped him up in her arms. Elvis seemed to melt into the crook of her neck and swooned at her as she talked to him.

"Why don't you take Elvis for a walk?" Emily was struggling to contain her joy. She ran to grab his leash and some treats when they agreed that would be a great idea. As the three of them headed for the shoreline, Emily could tell that Bella was conflicted. It had been a long time in cat years since Bella had Emily to herself, but based on her gaze down the beach, she wondered if Bella was missing her new friend.

"Don't worry, Bella. Elvis is staying in the family and will be visiting all the time."

Half an hour later, Emily could see the three of them walking back toward the cottage. Both Duncan and Jane had big smiles on their faces. Emily knew they'd fallen in love with Elvis, just like she and Anthony had done.

"He's amazing," Jane said as they walked up to the deck. "He's so athletic and friendly. Everyone we saw on the beach stopped to say hi to him."

"So, does that mean you're going to adopt him?"

Duncan began nodding and added a resounding, "Yes."

"Do the kids know anything about this?" Emily asked.

"Not yet. We wanted to talk to you first before we told them," Jane replied.

"I have a great idea. Sarah Klein is coming over tonight to visit and see Elvis before she returns to California. Why don't you bring the kids back while she's here? You can give them the good news and I think it would really help Sarah see Elvis with such a wonderful family. She's been struggling with the fact she couldn't bring him home because of her husband's allergies."

Duncan and Jane both agreed it was a brilliant plan. They'd pick up some pizza for everyone and would return after Sarah arrived. Jane thought it was best if Emily and Sarah could first talk in private, without distractions. It would also give Emily a chance to gather up all of Elvis's food, toys and dog bed. He was going to be sleeping in his new forever home tonight. Duncan and Jane were giddy as they left the cottage, eager to put their surprise plan for the kids in motion.

. . .

When Sarah arrived, there was a sense of calm about her, despite her tired appearance. After being inundated with wags and kisses, she picked Elvis up in her arms, hugging him tight. "I really needed this," Sarah said, referring to her visit with Elvis and Emily.

"How are you doing?" Emily asked. "I can only imagine you're dealing with a mix of emotions."

"I've gone from feeling angry and focused and then back to overwhelming heartache. The guilty parties will answer for their crimes, thanks to the hard work and dedication of everyone involved in finding my mom's killers. But I'm most grateful to you, Emily," Sarah said while reaching out to squeeze Emily's hand. "If you hadn't been there for my mom and Elvis and followed your own instincts, I don't think I'd have any closure. Thank you."

"I'm glad I could help. I have some great news that I think will lift your spirits. My brother and his wife, Jane, are going to adopt Elvis. With your blessing, of course. Their kids are madly in love with him, and I think it's mutual. You should see Elvis play with Mac and Ava. It's like he's smiling the whole time."

"Oh, Emily. That is the best news," and then Sarah sobbed. "I'm happy, really, and your family has been so kind. To be honest, there's a part of me that feels Elvis is my last connection to my mom. It's hard to let him go."

"I think it's safe for me to say that Jane and Duncan would welcome you anytime you want to visit Elvis." Emily could tell Sarah was comforted to know she wouldn't lose that permanent connection.

"When are they going to be bringing him to their home?"

"That's the best part. They're all coming over tonight and I thought you'd feel better seeing Elvis play with the kids. Jane and Duncan are going to wait to tell the kids when they're here."

"That's perfect. Thank you, Emily, for everything." Sarah gave Elvis one last squeeze before putting him back on the floor. He immediately ran over to give Bella a lick before jumping up on the couch.

"You had mentioned you're moving ahead to plan your mom's memorial service. Do you know what day it will be?" Emily needed to reconfigure her appointment schedule so she could block time off on the schedule.

"Yes, it's going to be Wednesday evening at my mom's house, and I want to make sure you can be there. Anthony too."

"Yes, we'll be there. If you need any help at all, please let us know."

"I'm going to set up some tents next to her beach deck so the service can be held outside. She loved living at the ocean and I know this would make her happy. Do you think Jane and Duncan could bring Elvis?"

"We'll ask them tonight, but I'm sure they'll be there if they can."

Emily was about to suggest they take Elvis for a short walk when Duncan, Jane and the kids arrived.

"Hi Auntie Em. We have pizza!" Ava announced. Right away, the kids were on the floor with Elvis. He was spinning and wagging his tail before fetching his soccer ball for them to play with. Their bond with Elvis was obvious to all.

"Kids, I want you to meet a friend of mine and a special friend to Elvis. This is Mrs. Sarah Klein," Emily said while making the introduction.

"Call me, Sarah."

"It's nice to meet you, Miss Sarah," Mac said. "You know Elvis?"

"I do. Elvis was my mom's dog, and she loved him very much. Your aunt has been so kind to take care of Elvis for me."

Based on his facial expression, Mac was struggling to understand why Elvis wasn't still with Mrs. Klein. A quick look exchanged between Jane and Duncan confirmed it was time to tell them.

"Kids, Miss Sarah's mom passed away recently and Auntie Em was taking care of Elvis until he could find his new forever home. How do you feel about Elvis becoming a member of our family?" Jane asked.

Both the kids stopped moving and turned and looked at their mom. Ava's eyes were as big as saucers and Mac asked, "You mean we can keep Elvis? Forever?"

"Yes, but you both have to promise you'll help to take care of him. That means feeding him, brushing him and taking him for walks."

"We will. We will," Mac and Ava shouted in unison while jumping up and down. Elvis joined in their celebratory dance, and Sarah was smiling while tears rolled down her face. Seeing Elvis in a loving home was the greatest gift.

Emily's visitors didn't stay long. The kids were excited to show Elvis his new home. Sarah promised Emily she would call her in the next couple of days and would send the memorial details tomorrow. Jane and Duncan were going to bring Elvis to Mrs. Klein's memorial service but were undecided if Mac and Ava would be there. They exchanged their contact info with Sarah and confirmed their commitment that she was welcome to visit Elvis whenever she wanted. Emily didn't get any additional details about the case from Duncan, but decided it could wait.

In an instant, the cottage became painfully quiet. The tumultuous past two weeks had been a powerful distraction from Emily's grief. She knew her mom would have been so happy to see the kids playing and bonding with Elvis.

"It's just you and me, Bella," Emily said. Bella replied with a diminutive meow and followed Emily onto the deck, jumping up to claim her rightful place on the chaise lounge. Emily thought of calling Anthony with the good news or checking her phone for any missed calls from Mike, but changed her mind. Everything else could wait until tomorrow. Listening to the gentle, rhythmic sound of Bella's purring was soothing and therapeutic. Tonight was all about closure, sunsets, and basking in the warm presence of her mom's memory.

CHAPTER EIGHTEEN

When Emily woke up Sunday morning, she was bombarded with a dozen texts featuring pictures of Mac, Ava and Elvis; playing, snuggling and bonding. Emily forwarded a few of her favorites to Sarah in case she was still feeling conflicted about saying goodbye to Elvis. There were two missed calls from Mike late last night, but he didn't leave a message. It was tempting to call him back, but a quick check of the time confirmed it was still too early. Besides, if it was something urgent, she was sure he would have left a message.

First things first. Emily was in desperate need of a cup of coffee before making any plans for the day. While the coffee was brewing, she grabbed the newspaper off the front porch. Her mom had always subscribed to the local weekend paper delivery, and this morning, Emily was glad she'd continued the tradition. With coffee in hand, she read the headline on the front page, *Local Realtor Charged with Murder*. Of course, she was already aware of most of the details of the story, but the criminal case against Richard Brant was more advanced than she realized. There were no details about Bucky's bail status, so Emily thought that would be a good reason to call Mike under the guise of getting an update.

While debating with herself whether it was socially acceptable to call at this early hour, Mike sent her a text asking if she could join him for lunch. He'd be around to pick her up at one o'clock and had a surprise to show her. Her answer was an obvious yes. It'd been a long time since Emily got butterflies about anyone she was dating.

A quiet knock at the door was alarming at this early hour until Emily saw Marc's car parked in the driveway.

"Morning, Em." Anthony said, while Marc greeted her with a bag of warm bagels.

"Anthony said you didn't have many groceries on hand, so we stopped by the local bakery on the way to our sunrise paddleboard yoga class."

"They smell delicious. Thanks. Can I get you guys a coffee?"

"No, we can't stay. Hey, where's Elvis?" Anthony asked while looking around the cottage.

"I have the best news. Jane and Duncan came over last night with the kids, and they've adopted him. Sarah Klein was here to see them all together, and it was magical. I know she's been dreading the day she had to say goodbye to Elvis, but she's so happy he's with Mac and Ava. And this way, she can see him whenever she wants."

"Yes," Anthony said, shouting out loud. "I was dreading the day Elvis found a new home, too. This is perfect."

"Sounds to me that Elvis was lucky to have both of you advocating for him," Marc said.

Anthony put his arm around Emily's shoulder and then gave her a high five with his free hand. "You did good, Em."

"I think you mean we did good." They both took a moment to celebrate their success.

Anthony and Marc left after a few minutes so they could get to their class on time. Emily used the rest of the morning to tie up some domestic loose ends—boring housework, laundry, brushing Bella and a quick trip to the grocery story. It was still too soon to consider placing a delivery order from Bengle's. Maybe one day soon she'd try again, but right now it invoked a little PTSD. After all that, it left her with just enough time to get ready for her lunch date with Mike. Today she felt like wearing her mom's coral-colored flip-flops. They were cheerful to look at and paired perfectly with her white tank dress.

Mike was right on time. "Hi, Emily," he said after greeting her with a light kiss on the lips. "You look really nice."

"Thanks. So, what's the big surprise?"

"Well, I need to show you first. Let's go." Emily followed Mike out the door, intrigued to find out what he had planned.

During their short ten-minute drive down the beach, Mike updated Emily on Mrs. Klein's case. Having been denied bail, Bucky and Richard Brant were now stuck behind bars awaiting trial. The judge had deemed Brant a flight risk based on his international connections and enormous wealth. Bucky admitted his role in the murder and was negotiating a plea agreement to flip on Brant, who was sheltered behind a wall of high-priced attorneys.

Mike already knew that Duncan had adopted Elvis since he was at Duncan's house last night for a brief visit and saw Elvis playing with the kids in a blanket fort they had built. Mike wouldn't say where he was taking Emily until he turned into a newer townhouse development. He glanced over at her and could see she was obviously confused, still in the dark about the purpose of their outing.

"Remember the other day I was telling you about a rental I was looking at? Well, I was going to sign the lease on this townhouse, but I wanted to get your opinion first."

Emily was beaming on the inside and out. Mike would now only be a short distance away, so she already loved the place. The realtor was waiting for them at the door and after a quick tour; the realtor left Mike alone to show Emily the outdoor spaces, including the beachfront pool.

"I know nothing can compete with the view from your place, but what do you think?" he asked.

"I think it's great. There's so much natural light, and the ocean views from your deck are amazing. I think you'll really love living on the beach."

He grabbed her hand in his and answered, "I already know I will."

The realtor had brought the paperwork for Mike to sign and starting the first of the month, this was his new home. Emily shouted a silent *yeah* to herself before they went to lunch to celebrate.

"I have to go into the station this afternoon to finish up some paperwork, but do you have any plans tonight?"

"No plans, but tonight is my turn to check the turtle nests. Do you want to join me?"

"Absolutely. I'll bring dinner. Seven o'clock?"

"Perfect."

Mike dropped Emily at home before returning to work. She spent the rest of the afternoon acting like a tourist in her own backyard. She carried her beach chair to the water's edge and then fell asleep reading one of her favorite mystery novels. It was a revelation to feel both settled and safe. She hadn't felt settled since her mom died and had not felt safe since Mrs. Klein's death. Helping Sarah deal with her grief had been both therapeutic and healing. Knowing she helped to put Bucky and Brant behind bars was the greatest reward of all. As each week passed by, Emily could now look back and see she was also processing her own personal loss.

The late afternoon sun was her cue to pack up the beach gear and get ready for her date with Mike. While checking her emails, Emily read through the details Sarah had sent about Mrs. Klein's memorial service. A notice was going to be placed in the local paper, and Emily was certain that most of the town would turn out for her service. Mrs. Klein was beloved, and the shocking news of her murder would be difficult for her friends to process. Emily forwarded the information to Anthony and thanked Sarah before confirming they would all be there. Sarah had also requested to speak with Emily late tomorrow. She had something important to discuss. Emily couldn't imagine what it could be, but of course, she would make herself available.

Mike was always punctual and arrived with grilled fish tacos from a famous local food truck. They ate quickly in order to get to their post at the turtle nests on time.

"I could really get used to this," Mike said while walking up the beach with Emily.

"You can join the Turtle Project anytime, you know. Marlon would be ecstatic."

"I mean, I could get used to walking on the beach with you."

"Oh. Me too." His candor surprised Emily. They held hands for the rest of the way and as they approached the first nest, they could see Marlon and Sharon standing together with a small group of volunteers.

"Hi, Emily. Nice to see you again, Mike," Marlon said.

"Hi. Did I get my dates mixed up? I thought I was on the schedule for tonight." Emily asked.

"No, it's your night. We agreed to meet up here when we heard about Eliza's murder. This was one of her favorite places, and it felt right to be here, plus we wanted to thank you in person. It's quite shocking, but it seems from the article in the paper you already knew about all of this. Are you okay, Emily?" Sharon asked.

"I'm okay, but thank you for asking." Emily wasn't named in the article, but anyone who knew her could infer that she was involved.

"And thank you, Mike, for working so hard to solve this crime. We owe you one for getting justice for Eliza."

"I was only doing my job. I regret I didn't know her," Mike replied.

"She was a force of nature," Sharon said. "She kept the rest of us in line and always had us laughing at the same time."

"What's going to happen to Elvis?" asked one volunteer.

"My brother and his family have adopted Elvis. He really bonded with my niece and nephew and he seems happy in his new home. Sarah Klein, Eliza's daughter, has been part of that decision too."

"Oh, that's wonderful. Elvis loves being the center of attention, and it sounds like a perfect home for him," Marlon said.

The group spent the rest of the night telling funny and heartwarming stories about Eliza while watching the nests for activity. They were fortunate to have a nest spring to life late in the evening. It was as if Eliza was there in spirit, encouraging the little hatchlings to safety.

It was later than usual when Mike and Emily made their way back to her cottage. They both had an early day tomorrow and were feeling the exhaustion from the past week. Mike made a point of asking Emily for another date before they melted into a steamy, passionate goodnight kiss. It would be great when they could get back to a normal routine and make plans to spend more quality time together. Until then, Emily was content with how things were going. Mike was almost too good to be true, and she was looking forward to see where things would go. While she was still curious about his previous romances, it didn't seem so important after recent life-altering events. She needed to stop living in the past, and maybe Mike felt the same.

■ ■ ■

The next morning, Emily was both shocked and pleased when she arrived at work to discover Anthony had stuck to their agreement and taken the day off. Emily missed him terribly, but knew he needed the break. She had a long call with Sarah Klein after work, and it took a concerted effort to stop herself from calling Anthony to share the news. She decided in the end she would keep some details to herself until Mrs. Klein's memorial service, which was scheduled for Wednesday evening right before sunset. It was monumental news, and she wasn't sure she could wait. It would be worth it to see the look on Anthony's face when he found out.

A day in the life of a veterinarian is anything but boring. Emily loved the challenge but now and then, she could really use a routine, almost mundane day with enough free time to collect her thoughts, spend time on the business aspect of running a busy hospital, and catch up with her patient follow-ups. It was that kind of day, and Emily had a feeling Anthony was involved in orchestrating a light schedule in his absence. There was even enough time for an actual lunch break, so Emily took advantage and ran a few errands.

She had more documents to drop off at the accountant's office and, truth be told; she wanted to see what was going on at the Good Life Realty Company. The local news channel had broadcast footage of a team of state investigators marching out of the realtor's offices with boxes and boxes of documents, computers, and who knows what else. Emily had to see for herself whether the threat had been neutralized.

"Dr. Benton, your first appointment after lunch has rescheduled, so you're free until Mrs. Palmer comes in with Otis for his follow-up x-rays," Abigail said while poking her head in the office.

"Perfect. I'm going out now and will be back in time for Otis. Thanks, Abigail."

Emily grabbed her keys and headed straight for her car. She only had to drop off the accounting documents, so she was in and out in five minutes. Despite feeling a little apprehensive about climbing the stairs to the third floor, the Good Life offices were dark and silent. There was a handwritten note on the door announcing that the offices were temporarily closed, offering a contact phone number to call with questions. If prospective clients needed any additional information about whether this was a reputable place to do business, there was police tape sealing the office doors. Emily felt no pity for Richard Brant. His greed caused his demise, and she hoped he would rot in jail. She couldn't help but think the other real estate employees, like the kind receptionist she'd met during her last reconnaissance mission, were innocent bystanders and now unemployed. There were many victims of his crimes.

"Nothing left to see here," she said to herself, followed by a heavy sigh of relief. The looming threat that had been hanging over her for a few weeks was truly gone. There was still time to run one fast errand. Emily wanted to buy a special outfit for Mrs. Klein's ceremony. Something cheerful to match the celebration of her life. A new pair of flip-flops or sandals would be in order as well since the event was going to be held on the beach in front of her home.

The little boutique was only a few blocks away from the hospital and always had something for those special occasions. Emily saw the perfect teal blue tank dress as soon as she walked into the store. It fit her perfectly, and the sales associate expertly matched it with sandals that were adorned with mini pearl-toned sea shells. During their last conversation, Sarah divulged she had called Mike, and he had agreed to attend as well. Another motivation for getting a new dress. She knew Jane and Duncan were going, but wanted to find out if the kids would be there.

"Hi, Jane. Do you have a minute to chat?"

"Sure, the kids are in school, and I'm on my way to the dog groomer. Where are you?"

"Just running a few errands at lunch. Have you decided whether to bring Mac and Ava to Mrs. Klein's celebration of life service?"

"Well, Duncan and I were talking about that this morning. Sarah called last night and invited us all. I was a little nervous about the kids attending a funeral at their age, but she convinced us it would be a joyful event on the beach. She really wanted Elvis to be there, and that's why I brought him to the groomer. Getting him all cleaned up for Wednesday."

"That's great. I'm glad you'll all be there. Sarah has a few announcements to make, and I wouldn't want you to miss it."

Before Jane could probe further, Emily told her she was pulling into the hospital and had to go. Otis would be waiting.

Otis was a ten-month-old beagle that was being seen for follow-up x-rays to ensure his broken toe had fully healed. It had been a ton of work for Mrs. Palmer to keep Otis's cast clean and dry and to restrict the playfulness of a young pup. Emily was happy to report she had been successful, and Otis could once again run and play—no more cast. It was always rewarding to deliver good news, but she had to bank those feelings for the days when she had to deliver difficult news to a loving pet parent. Lots of ups and downs in the life of a veterinarian, but that was par for the course.

Before Emily wrapped up her very productive day, she read a new email sent by Sarah Klein. It had more specific details about the surprise they were going to announce at the ceremony on Wednesday. That was the tipping point. There was no way Emily could keep this all to herself. She had to tell Anthony, and it would take all her willpower to wait until she saw him tomorrow morning.

CHAPTER NINETEEN

Wednesday was going to be one for the record books. Emily was cramming a full workday into a half day schedule so she could get to Mrs. Klein's celebration of life on time. Sarah Klein had some documents she wanted Emily to sign beforehand, and that was adding extra stress to the time crunch she was already dealing with. Emily had done her best to keep her secret about Sarah's announcement, but during the previous day at work, she couldn't hold it in any longer. While sitting in the office with Anthony, going over some hospital paperwork, Emily blurted it out. It was unplanned, but she couldn't help herself. Anthony had been tweaking the schedule to make sure they could leave early for the service and when she finished delivering the news, he sat there with his jaw hanging open and a look of shock on his face.

"Em, are you for real? Is this really happening?" he asked.

"It is. I know it's incredible. I couldn't believe it at first, but Sarah has worked out all the details over the past few days. Do you think we're taking on too much?"

"Not at all. This is an amazing gift for the whole Coral Shores community. I know Mrs. Klein worked hard to support all the local animal charities, but I never would have guessed it could lead to this."

Emily smiled and nodded. She'd been in awe of the generosity shown by both Sarah and Eliza Klein. This was going to change things forever.

. . .

Fifteen minutes before their early closing time, Abigail called back to the treatment area to ask if they could see a last-minute emergency. A prospective client had called about their puppy that had been vomiting all day. Anthony knew it would be a more serious appointment requiring the hospital to stay open later than planned. Puppies are always eating things they shouldn't and it can often result in an intestinal obstruction requiring hospitalization and surgery, or worse yet, they were at risk of contracting serious illnesses since their vaccinations weren't complete. Despite Emily's first instinct to say it was okay for the new client to bring in the puppy, Anthony convinced her, just this once, to recommend they take the puppy to the emergency hospital instead. There was a strong possibility they would have referred the puppy for overnight care and monitoring anyway, based on the information they received from the owner. Emily never turned away a patient, so it was difficult to say no, but being on time for Mrs. Klein's service was the absolute priority.

"I told the owners that if Freckle, that's the puppy, needs a recheck or further hospital care and x-rays, they can come back first thing in the morning without an appointment and we'll make them a priority. They're new to the area, and I think they felt better knowing there was a hospital they could come to for future care," Anthony told Emily.

"Did you explain this was a unique situation?" Emily asked.

"I did. I told them we were closing early to attend a funeral for a client, and Freckle's owner was even more impressed. Who wouldn't want that emotional connection and loyalty from their vet?"

"I guess that's true."

Anthony handed Emily her purse while motioning for her to stand up. "You better get going if you're to be on time to meet Sarah. I can close up here."

"Thanks, Anthony. She's coming by in an hour, and I want to take a few minutes to think about what I might say to everyone at the service once she makes her announcement."

"Just speak from your heart, Em." he said before forcing her out the back door of the hospital. They both had things to wrap up in order to be on time for Mrs. Klein.

...

While driving home, Emily reflected on everything that had happened in only a few short weeks. She was losing track while counting all the monumental life events that were piling up, one after the other. The murder of a beloved resident of Coral Shores had shocked the community, and everyone was thankful the guilty parties were now behind bars. Forget the fact that Emily had transitioned from being an innocent bystander to a witness, and then a victim, and even though nobody would say it out loud—a damn fine detective. It appeared she had a new boyfriend and had to admit she was smitten with him. Jane and Duncan now had a dog as a new member of their family. Elvis had worked his way into Emily's and Anthony's hearts and had taught them about unconditional love and resilience. Mac and Ava would now experience that same love. Emily knew Elvis would be the epic dog in the kids' lives. The dog at the center of all their future childhood memories. To top it all off, Emily and Anthony were about to embark on an exciting new endeavor. Just when Emily was getting her bearings on how to run a veterinary hospital, a whole new world was about to open up. She avoided thinking about all the work that would be involved. Now was the time to enjoy what was to come and what it could be.

Emily had an hour to freshen up, spend some quality time with Bella, and think about what she would say today if called upon to speak. "This is it, Emily. No turning back," she said out loud to herself, causing Bella to stare at her in confusion. Convinced it didn't involve her, Bella jumped down off the couch and moved to her elevated window perch. Emily thought perhaps Bella was getting used to her talking about nothing cat-related. Either that or she'd heard Sarah Klein's car pull into the driveway and wanted to move to a safe space.

"Hi, Sarah. Come on in," Emily said while opening the door.

"Thanks, Emily. And thanks for making time to see me today. I know you had to close the hospital early, and I hope that didn't create too many problems."

"Not at all. We had planned for it, so it worked out. Today is all about honoring your mom, and that's the only thing that matters."

For the first time since Emily had met Sarah Klein, she could talk about her mom without becoming overcome with grief. Proof that being able to say a proper goodbye brings essential closure. Emily was happy to notice the change.

"So, you mentioned you had some papers for me to sign?" Emily asked. She had already reviewed and approved the draft copy, so signing now was only a formality.

"Yes, nothing has changed from our final version. I'll give you a few minutes to review it, to be certain," Sarah replied.

"That's unnecessary. I'm jumping in with both feet because I trust you, Sarah, and I feel we'll make a great team to bring your mom's dream to life. It's my greatest honor that you're trusting me and Anthony with this important task."

"Emily, I can't think of anyone else to lead this project. I know I'm asking a lot of both of you, but I want you to know I've lined up all the support and specialists we'll need to reach our goals. I'm your partner in this to the end, but I'm going to rely on you to make all the important decisions about how we get there. The final decision will always be yours."

"Thank you, but I really see this as a collaboration. Anthony has skills I only wish to possess. I do have a vision of what it will look like in the end. With your help along the way, it's going to be amazing."

"I know it is too."

Emily signed the documents without hesitation—the final step before the service and the big announcement. She couldn't wait to see the expression on all the faces of Eliza's friends and colleagues when they heard the news. Sarah confirmed she was going to let Emily speak with everyone about her new role on her own terms. It was an enormous relief to find out she wouldn't have to give a speech today.

• • •

It was as if Eliza Klein wouldn't have stood for anything other than perfect weather for her service. Not a cloud in the sky, a light breeze, and a cool fresh evening by Florida standards. Emily noticed new flowers planted in front of Mrs. Klein's cottage. The interior was fresh and pristine, with all her personal effects safely packed up for Sarah to bring back to California. It was going to be difficult for Eliza's friends to be in her home without seeing her in it. By depersonalizing the cottage, it was easier to embrace the new venture to be announced later tonight. The patio deck had extra chairs for seating, and there was a handful of staff that were hired to assist with parking and handing out drinks and snacks. Sarah had rented a large white tent that was set up on the beach. It was filled with hanging baskets and pots overflowing with beautiful tropical flowers and had enough chairs to accommodate the sizable crowd that was expected tonight.

Emily saw Sarah standing inside the tent, conferring with someone she recognized as the minister that would be leading the ceremony. Pastor Doland supported Emily's mom during her illness and would be a familiar face for many of the locals attending.

He was a founding member of the Coral Shores Turtle Project before retiring and passing the mantle to Marlon. Also standing beside Sarah was a tall, distinguished looking man. Emily assumed he was Sarah's husband based on their body language and the intimate distance between them. Not wanting to interrupt, Emily waited on the deck.

"Emily, over here," Sarah waved for her to join them under the tent. Sarah introduced her husband, who then expressed his genuine gratitude for everything Emily had done to support his wife and Elvis. After a brief conversation, he excused himself so he could check on the staff to see if they needed any help. Emily thought he had kind eyes, and it was obvious in the way he looked at Sarah that he loved his wife and was very proud of her.

"Emily, how have you been?" asked Pastor Doland.

"Busy, mostly with work and the hospital," Emily replied.

"I think you've been busier than that. Sarah filled me in on everything you've been doing to protect Elvis and bring these murderers to justice. Thank you, Emily."

She smiled and nodded. "I'm happy to honor Eliza today."

Sarah grabbed Emily's hand and squeezed it tight. "I can't wait to tell all of her friends about our plans. Marlon and Sharon will be here soon. Do you know when Jane and Duncan are arriving with Elvis?"

"They should be here in a few minutes. Jane took Elvis to the groomer yesterday so he would look the part for his big reveal," Emily said.

Their conversation ended as the guests started to arrive and make their way onto the beach. Sarah made a point to greet every one of them personally. Her warm smile made it easy for the grief-stricken friends to embrace the fact that tonight was truly going to be a celebration of a wonderful life. It had been years since Sarah had moved away from Coral Shores, but her close relationship with her mother meant she had kept up on the details of their lives.

Emily wandered over to the deck to grab a cookie and a glass of lemonade from the buffet table and met Anthony and Marc, who were doing the same.

"This is quite the turnout," Marc commented. "It's clear she was a very special person."

"She was," Anthony replied and then turned to Emily and asked, "Are you nervous about tonight?"

"Well, maybe a little." Emily was feeling smothered by the outpouring of attention she received after the local paper and TV channel picked up the story. The spotlight intensified when the case became headline news and was broadcast to a national audience. Thankfully, the news cycle was short and things had quieted down.

It was a relief when Emily spotted her support team arriving. Jane, Mac and Ava walked onto the beach, followed by Duncan, who was leading Elvis on his leash. He was snowy white after his bath and seemed to have an elevated kick to his normal spunky gait.

"Auntie Em!" Mac waved and then ran up to her for a hug, followed by Ava. "Look at Elvis. He's so fancy. We got him a new collar and it has a bowtie on it."

"Wow, he does look fancy," Anthony said in agreement.

Jane and Duncan took a while longer to make it through the crowd as everyone in attendance stopped them so they could pet Elvis. Elvis was happy to be back in his old home with his new family, and it showed.

"Wow, Em," said Jane once they were all together. "There are so many people here."

"I'm not surprised. Everyone in this town loved her," Duncan said.

Right away, Emily saw Mike making his way from the house to where they were standing. Her face lit up in a way that caused Jane and Anthony to turn around to see who she was looking at before turning back, smiling at each other while gloating over their match-making success.

"You look beautiful, Emily. Hi, everyone," Mike said as he stood next to Emily and took her hand. "What a perfect night."

"It really is," Emily agreed. "I think Sarah is about to start the ceremony. Kids, do you want to walk Elvis over to say hi to Miss Sarah? She'd love to see his bowtie."

Ava and Mac were more than happy to show off Elvis. Sarah was delighted to see them together and told the kids she had saved special chairs for them to sit with Elvis at the front. Everyone began migrating into the tent to take their seats. This was a joyous affair, not a somber funeral. Friends were telling Eliza stories and laughing and hugging and remembering.

Pastor Doland gave a personal, heartfelt eulogy that brought tears and smiles to the faces of the Coral Shores community, who had gathered together to celebrate the life of a dear friend. He did not dwell on her tragic death, but on her life's accomplishments. During the ceremony, he singled out Duncan, Mike, Emily and Anthony for their special role in seeking justice for Eliza. Elvis received a blessing as he was embarking on his new life in a loving home. Everyone could tell that Pastor Doland was coming to the end of his tribute when he turned the ceremony over to Sarah to say a few words.

"Thank you to everyone for coming tonight to honor my mom. Your wonderful stories about her life show how important she was to you, and I know she loved you all in return. I felt my heart break in two when I received the call about my mom's death. It's been a difficult few weeks, but spending time back in Coral Shores with all of you has helped me to begin healing. Thank you for all your love and support. During our phone calls, mom always shared the wonderful stories about your lives, and I will forever feel connected to this community." Sarah took a minute to collect herself and wipe away the tears that were running down her face. There wasn't a dry eye to be seen. She took a deep breath, smiled, and then continued.

"As you know, my mom loved all creatures. She was involved with every local animal charity her entire life. Her deepest love was for her little dog, Elvis, and I can see tonight that you all know him well. The two of them spent many evenings on this beach, surveying the protected turtle nests to ensure they were safe and cared for. It was her wish that after she passed away, we would develop her home into a sea turtle conservation center that would serve her beloved community and bring generations of kids together in education. It was her lifelong dream. So, it's my pleasure to announce that tonight, you are all standing at the location of the future Eliza Klein Sea Turtle Education Center. An endowment was created to build a state-of-the-art facility. Dr. Emily Benton and Anthony Torres have agreed to be on the board of this foundation, and Marlon Bell and Sharon Whitaker will oversee day-to-day operations." While nodding at her honorees in the front row, she said, "Could you please stand up so we can show our appreciation for your dedication to this project?"

The crowd erupted in applause as the four of them stood to receive the adulation from their Coral Shores friends. Emily chuckled at the look on Anthony's face. He was beaming and confused, all at the same time. He knew he was going to be involved in the project, but did not know he had been named as co-director on the board with Emily.

Once the noise settled down, Sarah continued. "My mother held strong convictions that the beach should be accessible to everyone—not only for the wealthy people who could afford to buy and live here. For those of you who would like to walk your dog on the beach, an outdoor space will provide shade, water and a washing area to clean up after your outing. In order to keep the beach safe for the turtles, there will be directional signs to guide the dog walkers away from the fragile nests. You'll know what to look for since the signs will be easy to see and will feature an image of Elvis to mark the way. Mac, will you and Ava please join me up here with Elvis to show everyone what the signs will look like?"

Mac looked a little nervous, but was smiling as he walked to the front of the room with Ava and Elvis. Ava held his hand tight, but they both had one hand on Elvis's leash.

"Everyone, you'll be happy to know that Mac and Ava and their family have agreed to adopt Elvis. He's so happy in his new home. I'm sure you'll see them here often in the future. As most of you already know, this was Elvis's favorite place to be."

The guests all clapped, but a little quieter this time so as not to startle Elvis and the kids. Jane prompted them to wave at the audience and then they joined their parents back in their seats, beaming with pride.

Mac leaned over to whisper in Ava's ear. "Our dog has his own beach dog park. How cool is that."

"I'd like to invite you all to enjoy some refreshments and stay to watch this glorious sunset, in honor of my mom, Eliza Klein. Thank you for coming."

The crowd again erupted in applause. Quite a strange thing to happen at a funeral, but it really was a celebration of life and seemed like the natural thing to do. Emily could only imagine this joyful big party would please Eliza Klein.

Mac and Ava got to run around on the beach with Elvis while he chased his favorite sandpipers. Emily, Anthony, Marlon and Sharon were part of an unofficial receiving line that had formed so the guests could congratulate them on the new turtle center while offering their support. Marc was beaming with pride at Anthony, and while Jane and Duncan were at the water with the kids, Mike stood nearby, watching Emily shine.

As the guests had finished saying their last goodbyes, Emily was now surrounded by only her closest friends and family. They dragged their chairs to the ocean's edge to take in the last moments of the day. As the sun set on the horizon, they shared a unique communal feeling that tomorrow marked the start of something new. A future filled with family—both two and four-legged, love, friendship, hard work and joy. Emily could ask for nothing more.

ABOUT THE AUTHOR

DL Mitchell is the author of *Trust the Terrier: A Coral Shores Veterinary Mystery* and a practicing small animal veterinarian. After working in busy hospitals in Miami and Northern Virginia, she opened a veterinary house call practice, offering concierge care for her feline and canine patients in the Atlanta area. On a daily basis, she is inspired by the bond between her clients and their furry family members. Their amusing and heartwarming stories inspire the true-life cases showcased in *Trust the Terrier*.

She enjoys spending time with her husband and daughter and their menagerie of pets, planning their next travel adventure, and running on nearby trails.

DL Mitchell is an active member of the Atlanta Chapter of Sisters in Crime and the Atlanta Writers Club.

NOTE FROM DL MITCHELL

Word-of-mouth is crucial for any author to succeed. If you enjoyed *Trust the Terrier*, please leave a review online—anywhere you are able. Even if it's just a sentence or two. It would make all the difference and would be very much appreciated.

Visit my website at DLMitchellMystery.com for information about book signings, new releases, and more.

Thanks!
DL Mitchell

We hope you enjoyed reading this title from:

BLACK ◆ ROSE
writing™

www.blackrosewriting.com

Subscribe to our mailing list – *The Rosevine* – and receive **FREE** books, daily deals, and stay current with news about upcoming releases and our hottest authors.
Scan the QR code below to sign up.

Already a subscriber? Please accept a sincere thank you for being a fan of Black Rose Writing authors.

View other Black Rose Writing titles at
www.blackrosewriting.com/books and use promo code
PRINT to receive a **20% discount** when purchasing.